J.T. Lions has worked in financial services for over two decades, and his debut novel draws upon his personal insight as a trader dealing with wealthy clients in a private bank in London.

Having borne witness to some of the most unbelievable and scandalous events to hit the financial sector in modern history, these experiences prompted him to focus on financial crime as a theme for his story.

Although he is an accomplished amateur artist, writing has become his new hobby. He plans to write a sequel…there is no shortage of murky characters in the financial underworld!

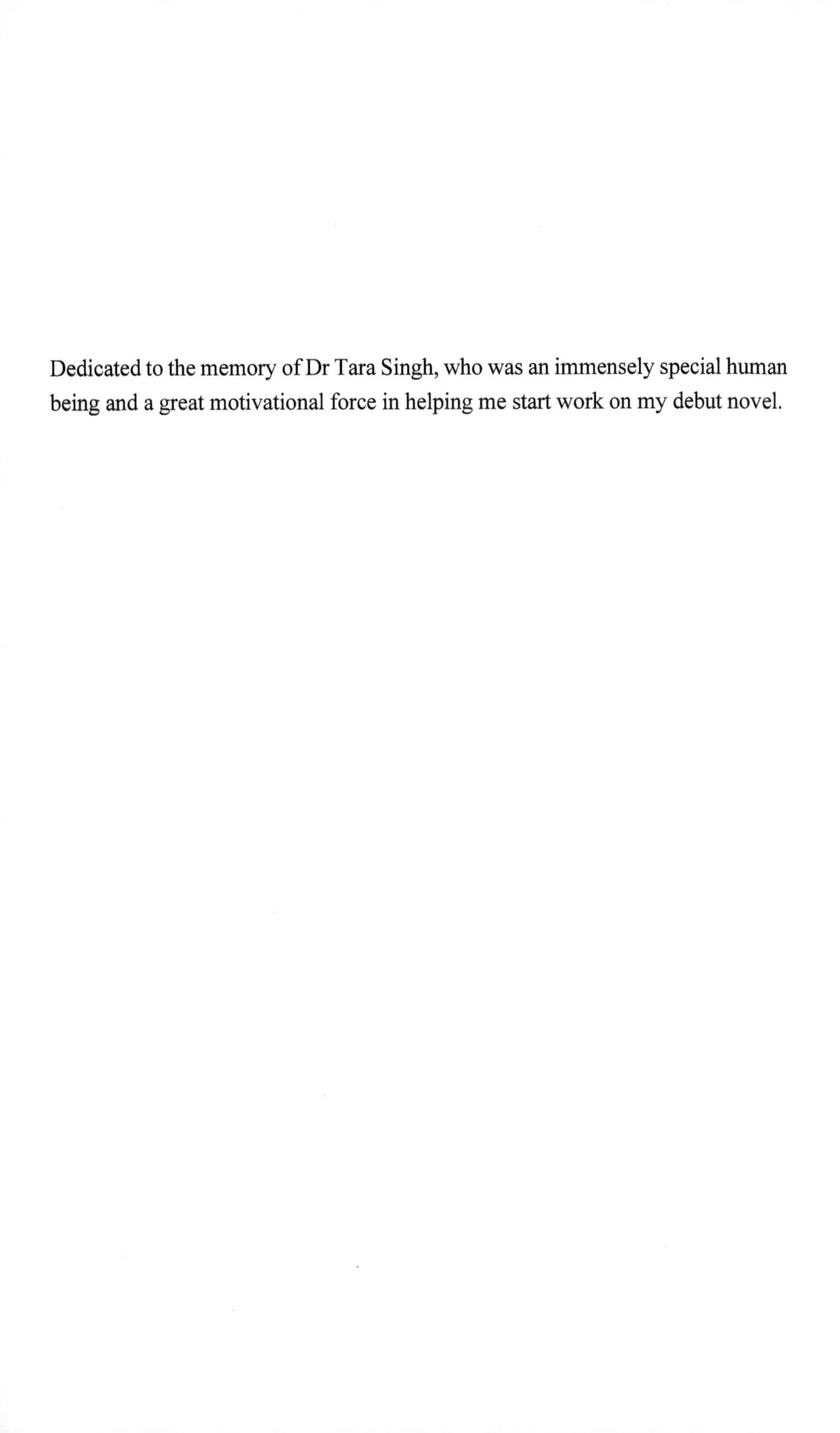

Dedicated to the memory of Dr Tara Singh, who was an immensely special human being and a great motivational force in helping me start work on my debut novel.

J.T. Lions

THE IDENTITY KIT

AUSTIN MACAULEY PUBLISHERS™
LONDON * CAMBRIDGE * NEW YORK * SHARJAH

This is a work of fiction. Names, characters, businesses, places, events, locales, and incidents are either the products of the author's imagination or used in a fictitious manner. Any resemblance to actual persons, living or dead, or actual events is purely coincidental.

A CIP catalogue record for this title is available from the British Library.

ISBN 9781398482524 (Paperback)
ISBN 9781398482531 (Hardback)
ISBN 9781398482555 (ePub e-book)
ISBN 9781398482548 (Audiobook)

www.austinmacauley.co.uk

First Published 2024
Austin Macauley Publishers Ltd®
1 Canada Square
Canary Wharf
London
E14 5AA

A special thank you goes to my awesome wife, Nikki. Not only was she helpful in reading early drafts, but she also gave me continuous encouragement. She was invaluable just being herself and acting as a source of inspiration for the lead female character!

Table of Contents

Chapter 1
The V.I.P. Meeting

"My love for you is a journey; starting at forever and ending at never," announced my fiancée.

I stopped typing on my laptop, my mind distracted. I wasn't sure whether it was the majesty of what had just been uttered or the sudden realisation of the union to which I was going to be bound. Thoughts of serenity, love and children playing in a garden filled my head.

"What a lovely quote!" I responded, whilst attempting to contemplate its deeper meaning. Before my mind could return to whatever I was typing, I was distracted again, this time by a jeering crowd outside my second-floor apartment.

It had been a calm Sunday evening until that point. Earlier I had gone to the park for a jog and was now preparing for an important meeting at work tomorrow. Nancy, my fiancée, was busy perusing 'wedding planner' websites in preparation for the big day next month.

"Over here!" I heard a man shout.

"Can you answer one question?" shrieked another.

"Just one shot, sir," exclaimed someone else.

The constant shouting from street level forced me to enquire further. Hastily peering out of the window, I saw a large crowd of paparazzi gathered around the entrance of my apartment block. There was the usual jostling and shuffling and flashes of light and at its epicentre, I caught sight of a suited man, exiting a chauffeured car with a couple of burly aides. He entered the building, smiling at the porters who were holding the front doors open. He said nothing to the horde of photographers grappling for his attention; instead, leaving one of his bodyguards to exchange a few unfriendly words with them. At first, I didn't recognise him, but then I remembered his image from a recent news bulletin.

Yes, I pondered, *that's him, the new manager of Chelsea football club.* My curiosity had been satisfied, and I took no further interest. In fact, in my building I saw famous residents all the time, particularly Members of Parliament, as the corridors of power were only a few streets away, but other inhabitants included a few people you could call TV personalities.

"What's the commotion about, Josh?" asked Nancy from the sofa.

"Oh, it's the new manager of Chelsea," I replied. "Arriving with the usual chaos of the press."

"I see; I read that he was going to rent in the area," she said.

"What is it about this place? There's always a resident in the newspaper for some reason or another! A week doesn't go by without journalists swarming around the foyer; I'm going to ask for a discount on my service charge!"

The noise outside didn't last long, and I sat down to resume the preparation for my meeting. Actually, it was an investor appraisal followed by a business lunch with my most revered client, Mr Alain Bertrand. He was a prominent figure in the business world, but known more so for being a member of European royalty and arguably more famous than any football manager or TV personality.

Nancy and I spent the remainder of the evening watching TV, and when the 10 o'clock news had finished, I decided to retire to bed. Before doing so, I looked through the living room window again. Outside, it was surprisingly quiet, apart from a solitary figure waiting at the bus stop below. My particular abode faced Marsham Street, a rather innocuous but upmarket street in Victoria, London. It consisted of three bedrooms and a generous lounge, in one of the most prestigious residential developments in the area. It was the first to have two communal swimming pools, bulletproof windows in the penthouses and a media room. The concierge facilities and valet parking were perfectly suited to my hectic lifestyle as a client services professional in a well-known hedge fund. But this luxury came at a price, a mortgage that would destine me to client service meetings for a very long time!

The following morning, I put on my best business suit and hurriedly left the apartment to get to work. Passing through the foyer, I gave a quick nod to the concierge as he opened the door for me. I stepped onto a sunlit pavement, the brightness made me wince, but I was greeted by a refreshing breeze. The valet, who was lining up cars for several of the residents, waved in my direction to which I responded with a smile.

My office was located on Pall Mall, a major thoroughfare in the West End and only a short stroll for me across St James's Park. As I crossed the park at this early hour, a scurry of squirrels playfully jumped over flowers and scrambled up trees. The brownish-green footpath from last autumn's leaf fall had been cleared with the arrival of spring. The lake in the middle glistened with the morning light, and for a moment I forgot about the tribulations of my meeting and basked in the glory of the moment. It was going to be a fine day.

I got to my office, which was housed in one of the grand mansions adorning the stretch of road heading towards Trafalgar Square. From my desk on the top floor, I could see St James's Palace, which crowned Pall Mall at the other end as it turned upwards towards Piccadilly. The rest of my view comprised of the green expanse of the park and the landmarks of Westminster and beyond.

After a couple of hours of uninterrupted work, the security desk gave me a courtesy call that Mr Bertrand had arrived and was on his way up. I rushed to the lift lobby ready to greet him, whilst my mind replayed all the key questions I had prepared for yesterday; there was no margin for error with this client.

The lift opened and there he stood, a confident, assured man, his dark hair neatly pressed against his head. He looked at least five years younger than his real age of forty-five. Dressed in a blue tailored suit and wearing a diagonal patterned tie, handmade shoes completed his look as he stepped forward with a smile honed from years of official business.

"Alain, it's a real pleasure to see you again," I said.

"Always nice to see you too, Josh."

"How are you enjoying your stay in London?"

"Very well, London in late spring is such a lovely place."

"Oh yes, it is," I said, as we began walking towards the meeting room. "Seeing anyone interesting on this trip?"

"In fact, yes, I've been invited to the French Embassy tonight, for a dinner hosted by President Sarkozy."

"Wow!" I said. "What a great invitation!"

We arrived at the meeting room, and I gestured to Mr Bertrand to enter. The room's eighteenth-century interior had been preserved magnificently and befitted a Grade II listed building, apart from a video conferencing unit tucked into a corner of the room. Although other meeting rooms on our premises were modernised and devoid of their original features, the entire building exuded an archaic charm. Inside the antiquated room, everything was laid out as expected. Beverages and pastries were left on a sideboard, sheets of paper and writing instruments embossed with the company logo were placed at two settings on the mahogany table in the centre of the room, and the video conferencing unit was switched on. Such opulence was meant to impress, to show clients they were dealing with the best of the best. As Mr Bertrand sat down, he instantly noticed one of the paintings had been replaced. "Ah, I really liked the grey horse," he muttered. "Why the change?"

It made me think and interrupted my flow. "I think 'the horse' may have been from David Highfield's personal collection." David was the Chief Executive Officer of Omega Centurion Investments, the company for which I worked. Having graduated from Oxford with a Physics doctorate, he was one of the early pioneers to have applied the social sciences to the art of investing, and in doing so spawned one of the leading companies of its generation. Owning a majority stake in Omega, David was often quoted in global rich lists but was reserved in his spending habits; collecting art was his only vice.

We helped ourselves to some coffee and biscuits and then got down to business. I turned to Mr Bertrand and began my pitch, conscious of looking concerned and empathetic. "In today's meeting, I'd firstly like to talk about the poor economic environment and the losses suffered by almost all our industry. We can then discuss the negative returns on your investment portfolio and how our strategy is affected in this part of the business cycle. Finally, we can talk about some of the new funds we have on offer." I was hoping that emphasising the dire state of the economy and the current fiscal problems, it would put his diminishing portfolio size into context.

"The thing is Josh, I understand that difficulties have arisen with the tightening of credit due to the silly lending practices of the past. This has caused people to withdraw money from all types of investments and hoard their cash, but you are an absolute return manager. Your company prides itself on making money no matter what the circumstances, boom or bust. Deteriorating investment returns will force a redemption on some of my investment with Omega, and I might possibly hold more cash, even invest elsewhere."

He was right, I thought to myself, and the word 'redemption' was almost akin to a swear word in my industry. Less money to manage would mean lower commissions for the firm and smaller bonuses for people like me! I immediately thought about my forthcoming wedding expenses, I desperately relied on this client's investment; this meeting had to go well!

"Our trading strategy has been stress tested with this type of scenario, the investment managers feel we can profit if the current trends continue. We have been adding to our gold positions and buying government treasuries due to perceived demand." I voiced.

"But you and I both know that we cannot go on past performance, today we have a situation where ordinary people are facing misery from job losses and reduced pay. Some have unfortunately lost their homes and this climate is one that many generations have not faced. Testing is based on assumptions and today no one knows what those are."

Again he was right; there were uncertainties out there that simply no one knew. Times were as difficult as anyone could remember. But I had to get a positive message across and make this client feel good about the company. It was time to use a few sales tricks of mine, starting with changing the topic. "Things are bad," I admitted. "And there are unknowns out there, but the world is changing, there is a sea change of thinking out there. Just look at Obama, for the first time since Reagan does a US President have the ear of the masses, such political goodwill. He has enough clout to change the situation around."

"Absolutely, the US election was a marvellous thing; it shows people can overcome the odds, did you see the crowds in Washington? They were magnificent and well deserved for such a fine fellow."

"Yes, it was a thrill to watch, although I don't entirely agree with some of his party's doctrine," I said. "Do you think a four-year term is sufficient time for the administration to turn things around?"

"It depends, it's down to the political will of his party, they need to work as a team, have an *esprit de corps* as they say in France."

My technique was working, I thought, *the discussion was taking another path.* But, suddenly, Mr Bertrand returned to the difficult question. "I'm still keen to know why the last six months have been so challenging for this company. One of your competitors, New Trend Advisors, has managed to hold on to its profits. They've almost made double-digit returns rather than losses."

This was precisely the name I didn't want to hear, they had done splendidly well out of the proverbial mess the economy was in. "New Trend Advisors have defiantly outperformed, and praise goes to their investment management team.

But you've got to remember they've only been around five years or so, our firm has a track record stretching back almost thirty years."

"They might be new kids on the block but what they're doing has got to be admired," he replied.

Feeling slightly frustrated, I nodded with solemn agreement. It was time to employ my second sales tactic, get the client to talk about themselves. "By the way, I read in the paper that you were part of a consortium that bid for the bankrupt music retailer Spacey, how did that go?"

"Oh, that turned out to be a sad affair. The company ran up large debts and couldn't sustain its operations. Fundamentally, it was a sound business with a niche place in the music world. We put in a proposal to get rid of all the board members who collectively were incompetent and keep floor staff redundancies to a minimum, but the greed of their management team meant that they'd rather let the company fold. The consortium tried its best but was unsuccessful, it was a shame, two thousand people were laid off," he said, gazing down at the table, pensive in thought.

"Sorry to hear that. What it highlights is that companies aren't making the right decisions for the long term, the short-term philosophy of companies needs to change."

"Indeed, I see your point," said Mr Bertrand emphatically, "but everyone's in the same situation. It's a fair playing field out there. You have exactly the same information at your disposal as does your competitor New Trend. It seems their analysis and insight have been spot on recently."

I had to downplay the recent good performance from New Trend, so it was time for sales tactic number three, to play on a client's fears. "I agree we're in the same situation, but to reiterate the point I made earlier on, this company has a trading approach that's been tested with real client money over a very long time, we've seen downturns and weathered the storm. New Trend might have had an edge over us in the last six months, but no one knows how their approach will work going forward. Omega did well during the technology bubble crash as well as the recession of the early nineties. We've faced these tumultuous situations and prospered; we're a big company with large resources; and I would question how many of these new start-ups will be around in five years' time?"

Before Mr Bertrand could answer, there was a knock at the door. "Come in," I said.

David Highfield entered the room and we stood up to greet him. "Alain, it's so nice to see you again," he said, and then turned to me, "sorry for interrupting your meeting, Josh, but I was just passing by." Facing back to Mr Bertrand he continued, "I hope you are being well looked after, how are Penelope and the children?"

"Very well thank you," replied Mr Bertrand. "And how is Joan?"

"She's fine thanks; in fact, she's helping organise our golf charity day, has Josh told you?"

"Ah no, we were still in the middle of discussing…technical matters," he said diplomatically. "A charity day sounds fantastic!"

"Yes, it's a one-off opportunity to play amongst some of the greats. We're sponsors of the event, hopefully Tiger Woods and Nick Faldo will be in attendance!"

"What an opportunity!" exclaimed an excitable Mr Bertrand.

"It's at the Grove, where Woods triumphed in 2006. Are you familiar with the course?"

"I know the place, it is in Hertfordshire no? I haven't played there yet."

"Good, now's the chance, anyway, we'll have a chat a bit later on," said David, reaching for the door.

"Certainly, au revoir."

As David left I noticed that Mr Bertrand was still ruminating about the golf day. His interruption couldn't have been better timed.

"I think it's commendable this company puts a generous proportion of its profits towards good causes," said Mr Bertrand. "The question I have to ask myself is where do I put my money right now? Should I keep all my money with the company in which I have placed immense trust, or diversify and see what the new kid on the block can do? I can tell you that I'm undecided, Josh."

"Do you know how long it takes to send a trade electronically on a computer network and execute a client transaction?" I asked.

Slightly bewildered, he began musing about a response. "I'm not sure, probably a few milliseconds."

"The average speed is five milliseconds in our industry. Do you know how much a one-millisecond network delay can cost this company on every deal?"

"I'm not sure, and I don't understand the point you're making."

"The cost is approximately seven dollars on every deal. It doesn't sound like much, but it all adds up given the volume of trades that we do. One initiative we're working on is to physically locate our trading computer servers next to the exchanges and markets on which we trade. Our computer systems will see market orders much faster than other participants, and in theory, beat our competitors in getting the best prices by being the first in the queue. This could save tens of millions of dollars in commission every year. If we'd done that six months ago, our performance would have been in line with New Trend."

"Interesting," he remarked.

"I'm telling you this because it's an example of how we innovate, how we always maintain an edge over our competitors." I was getting fairly spirited now. "In fact, we've got an army of scientists, engineers and mathematicians working on that right now. We may well not be at the top of the performance league every quarter, but you know damn well over the long run we'll be there!" I paused and there was silence. Mr Bertrand glanced at the spot where the painting of the grey horse had been, and we both looked at its modernist replacement. It was by an Impressionist—Cezanne I recalled.

"I like it," smirked Mr Bertrand. "Simple yet cunning." His reaction took me aback. "Maybe I shouldn't lose faith. The thing is Josh I do trust your judgement. Why don't we see how the fund performs over the next half-year; hopefully, things will improve."

"That's been my point," I said, feeling the tension of the morning evaporate from my mind. Conscious that he may have probed me a bit more on what we'd discussed so far, I moved straight to the last item on the agenda. "Now we still need to discuss the new issues and fund launches we have to offer."

"I'm conscious of the time—why don't we review those over lunch," he said.

"Good, I'll take you to see Miles for an update from the Trading department. Remember he's coming to our lunch too."

"Oh, really?" Mr Bertrand sighed. "He is a very nosey man, can you believe he asked me about the takeover of Spacey and whether we were going to float its music app? Insider information was my reply!"

"Too right," I said. "He should know better than to ask such questions."

With the main points covered, we got up and exited the room. I felt like I'd already worked the entire day, but was satisfied with the outcome and left Mr Bertrand with Miles.

Chapter 2
Lunch at the Golden Orchid

Several hours later I met Mr Bertrand outside the lift area. His meeting with Miles had been more of a social chat than a business engagement from what I gathered, presumably steered that way by him to avoid any difficult questions.

"So, I've booked the Golden Orchid for lunch. Miles said he'll join us in a short while. Have you been to its sister branch in Hong Kong, it's very authentic?" I asked.

"No, but this lunch is just what I've been craving," said Mr Bertrand as we began walking towards St James's Square. I hosted client lunches once or twice a week, and they provided a nice break from gobbling a sandwich at my desk. Other departments in the company were mildly envious of this sales perk; however, client lunches were no feast. It was still business.

"I bet you're looking forward to meeting the President this evening?"

"Before he was elected, I met him several times. He is a pleasant man and very lucky, he must be if he's married to Carla Bruni!" I laughed in agreement. I could only imagine the pomp and ceremony of the dinner that Mr Bertrand was due to attend. For most people, it would be the ultimate dinner invitation, although for him it was a regular event in his well-connected life.

We took a sharp left at the top of the square and arrived at the restaurant. It covered the ground and basement area of a modern building encased between two Victorian houses. The discrete red and gold exterior blended in tastefully with its surroundings and had all the hallmarks of an upmarket joint. Mr Bertrand seemed impressed, Golden Orchid already had a Michelin star; rumour had it that it was being awarded a second.

The head waiter turned around and caught my eye, gently gesturing for me to wait as he finished talking to a smartly dressed gentleman who was holding a large notepad.

"If the kitchen inspection is what I expect it to be, my report will be very complimentary," said the gentleman. "This restaurant lives by the highest standards. The ambience and décor are a dream, the clientele sophisticated," as he looked approvingly at Mr Bertrand. "It's simply a routine inspection. You did receive advance notice a couple of days ago?"

"Yes, Mr Cuthbert-Jones," replied the waiter. "I have the letter from the Food Inspections Agency right here and you are welcome to carry out your assessment."

"Well, thank you very much," said the inspector as he was led away by another member of staff. Despite the small delay incurred, my client seemed pleased to have overheard the conversation.

"Good afternoon, Mr Rosenburg," said the waiter finally turning to me, "sorry about the wait."

"No problem, Sven. Hope you're well. I have a table at half-past for three people."

"Your table is ready, would you like a drink at the bar while you wait for the other person?"

"Sure."

The ground floor bar area was populated by a predominately suited crowd. More casual dinners were also lounging around but everyone seemed to be talking business. The leather couches were taken, but I spotted a few empty stools at the end of the bar and we made our way through the mob of bodies.

"What would you like to drink?" I asked.

"Hmm, let me see, a glass of champagne would be nice," said Mr Bertrand inspecting the drinks menu. "Quite a nice selection I must say. I'll go for the Krug '08." I ordered his drink and got a gin and tonic. "Good to see this is one restaurant still defying the downturn. One of my favourite eateries in Paris has closed down. It was run by a celebrity chef, however, the trend amongst an increasing number of people is to limit eating out, and treat themselves to a gourmet ready meal at home instead."

"The same is happening over here; supermarkets are muscling in on premium convenience food," I said. "And what about Prosecco! Looks to have dented the Champagne market."

"Capitalism is ruthlessly efficient, if you can't supply the right product at the right price, the consumer will punish you."

I was about to raise one of the unfinished items from the meeting but before I could begin, I noticed a man walking towards us. It wasn't Miles, and he had his eyes fixed on Mr Bertrand. He looked of South European appearance with tanned skin and dark hair, but otherwise, his features were not prominent.

"Mr Bertrand?" the stranger enquired.

"Yes," he said, with a look that suggested he failed to recognise the face.

"My name is Daniel Joubert. I met you at the Paris Business Fair last year." The stranger spoke with a French accent.

"Ah yes monsieur, I was there."

"We were talking about investment in Asia and golf courses in Scotland," said Mr Joubert.

"Ah I vaguely remember," said Mr Bertrand, out of politeness rather than any concrete memory. "Talking about golf is one of my pastimes." They both laughed. "Are you attending the business fair this year?"

"Most probably; it provides a good opportunity to talk to businesses directly and it's a showcase for up-and-coming companies, including my new launch called Joubert Design."

"I see, so we may meet again?" Mr Bertrand asked.

"Maybe—I'll look out for you. By the way, do you know how I can get to the Institute of Directors on Pall Mall?"

I politely interjected, "The Institute is only a few buildings away from here." I looked outside the glass front of the restaurant and began giving directions.

"Thank you," he said and then faced Mr Bertrand. "Nice meeting you, au revoir."

I waited until the stranger had got beyond earshot. "I take it you didn't recognise the man?"

"No," chuckled Mr Bertrand.

My phone suddenly rang, and I took the call which only lasted a few seconds. "It's Miles, he won't be able to make it for lunch and sends his apologies."

"That's fine and bit of a relief! Shall we go to our table?"

We finished our drinks and the head waiter showed us to a table near the stairs. The dining area was decorated in carved wood and bamboo, with the menu also inscribed on a bamboo tablet.

"The scallop tempura sounds tempting."

"It does," endorsed Mr Bertrand.

"And for mains, for me, it's a choice out of the aromatic lamb or chilli shredded Wagu beef. How about drinks? Shall we get a bottle of Krug Grande Cuvée?" I said knowing it would impress.

"I'll stick to water. I've got a big evening ahead of me, plus I don't want to break your expense account!" he joked.

The service was brisk and efficient, before we could get stuck into any particular talking point the starters had arrived. "Sure looks good," I said.

Mr Bertrand delicately sliced a scallop after examining the minimalist arrangement on his plate. Having the air of a MasterChef judge, he took a small mouthful. "*Très Bien,*" he pronounced. The overpriced menu didn't appear such bad value after all! "If only someone could replicate this type of Chinese cooking in Paris, they'd make a fortune."

"Too bad my money's tied up in a dodgy doughnut joint," I muttered.

"Doughnut joint?"

"Oh, I was thinking aloud," I said. "I've invested a large sum in a doughnut chain in London. As it happens it's being sued because someone slipped on a doughnut and injured themselves! Allegedly it's the shop's fault." Mr Bertrand smirked at the comment. "Yes, apparently the generous sugary coating on the Raspberry Mocha is to blame and it's a health and safety issue!"

"Slipped on a doughnut…," laughed Mr Bertrand.

"Sounds silly I know." I was seeing the funny side of the story. "Well, I have a stockbroking friend who makes all sorts of crazy recommendations, and he suggested I invest before it floated on the stock exchange. Apparently, its sales strategy is to come up with quirky flavour combinations, they sell a vodka and banana flavour with mint sprinkles!"

He laughed even louder, and then unexpectedly, his eyes opened really wide. The gleeful look on his face gave way to a painful flinch. His lips began to swell and he grabbed his throat, something wasn't right.

"Are you okay?" He began coughing and was still holding his throat. The waiting staff turned around with concern. "Mr Bertrand, are you okay?" I shouted. The coughing got louder and his face started swelling too. "He's not well!" I yelled to the nearby staff. In a panic, two waiters ran to the table, but at this point, his face already resembled a large watermelon. His cheeks were flush, and he was closing his eyes, evidently in excruciating pain.

"He's having an allergic reaction," shouted one waiter, "get the EpiPen!"

"Are you sure?"

"Yes, I've been trained in first aid and seen it before, look at the way his lips and face are swollen."

My heart skipped several beats, and I stood there in disbelief. This wasn't happening. Mr Bertrand started shaking violently. "Help!" He squealed, with his head now flat on the table. I began supporting him in his chair. Beads of sweat were breaking out over my body and the whole restaurant abruptly stopped and stared. One waiter disappeared into the kitchen, and we must have been waiting two minutes before he re-emerged with an injection. By this time, an army of staff and onlookers were surrounding our table.

"I've called for an ambulance," one of the diners shouted.

"Stand back," the waiter announced, "I'm a first aider. I'm going to inject the EpiPen."

Mr Bertrand was now unconscious and a strange colour. The injection was administered but there was no reaction; my prized client lay there, motionless and comatose.

It wasn't long before the ambulance arrived. The medical crew rushed towards our table and tried to resuscitate Mr Bertrand. Being unsuccessful, they put an oxygen mask around his face and attached various tubes to his body. Then they placed him on a stretcher and took him carefully into the rear of the ambulance. I just stood there at the table, a witness to the most unfortunate event that had ever happened to me. A complete tragedy had unfolded, and I had been powerless to help. All my intricate planning for the meeting could not have foreseen this terrible eventuality. What was I going to do? Should I call work or go to the hospital? These thoughts were racing through my mind when the restaurant manager approached me.

"Would you like some water, sir?"

"Please," I said, taking a seat nearby and loosening my necktie.

"What happened?"

"He started coughing and then...he had some sort of adverse reaction."

"Would you mind staying here for a while? I need to write a report for health and safety," the manager said.

"Yes, I can." The manager queried our lunch order and asked other basic questions. It appeared he was covering his back in case there was any chance of litigation against the restaurant. After ten minutes of questioning, I saw a policeman walking towards us, which startled me. He called the manager to one side and they had a brief discussion.

"Everyone, can I have your attention? The incident is over. Please can you get on your way," the policeman announced.

The manager of the restaurant then stepped in. "We will speak to each table to sort out the bill, there will be a concession because of events. Please bear with us while we work through everyone." The waiters began negotiating bills with several customers but one or two diners had already walked off.

"I can't believe what's just happened," I said randomly to the people that were still standing around.

"What exactly happened?" someone asked.

"I don't know, it seemed like an allergic reaction. He was a man in good health," I replied.

"Can I remind people to go on their own ways now," shouted the policeman again. "I'd like a quick chat if you please," said the policeman looking at me.

The crowd began dispersing. "There's a room at the back, you can speak in there," said the manager. I didn't know what to think or how to feel, I followed the policeman into the room.

"I need to take some details sir, it is routine procedure," he said.

"Sure."

"What's your name?"

"Joshua Rosenburg."

"Address?"

"Flat 15, St Andrew's Residences, Marsham Street, Westminster."

"Place of work?"

The questions continued in a similar vein to what the restaurant manager had asked. After fifteen minutes, I was free to go. Shall I go straight to the hospital? What should I say at work? I thought it was best to call the office rather than pop in and face another onslaught of interrogation. I called reception and Stacey, the receptionist, answered the line.

"Hello Josh."

"Hi Stacey, I wanted to let you know that I may not be coming back to the office this afternoon. During my client lunch, Mr Bertrand fell ill and was taken to hospital."

"Oh, sorry to hear that, anything serious?"

"Er, I'm not sure, but I'm going to St Thomas' to see how he's doing."

"Okay, is there anything I can do?"

"Please let David Highfield know and," I paused for a second, "it might be worth informing the French Embassy. Mr Bertrand has an important dinner there this evening."

"Shall I attempt to call his wife?"

"Yes, that's a good idea, David should have her number."

Mr Bertrand lay in the ambulance and the paramedic turned to the driver. "He's unconscious, but at least he hasn't gone into anaphylactic shock."

"Do you think the EpiPen did the trick?" the driver asked.

"Yeah, I reckon it helped. The waiter did a good job."

"He was probably the one that served this unfortunate chap maggot-laden grub in the first place!" the driver chuckled.

"Looked like a nice joint though," said the paramedic.

"Nah, their kitchen probably tells a different story."

"I take it you're not going to dine there with your missus?" the paramedic asked.

"No, but that's because I don't fancy taking out an unsecured loan just to have dinner."

"Walkin' in there made me kinda peckish, fancy a Chinese takeaway after the shift?" the paramedic asked, searching Mr Bertrand's pockets for some ID.

"Yeah, good idea," replied the driver.

The paramedic came across Mr Bertrand's French driving licence in his wallet. However, there was another plastic card next to it that caused him to jump. He'd seen it once before. "He's got one of those diplomatic passes, you know, that government officials have."

"You're joking!"

"No, this guy is some kinda VIP. I think we better call the hospital again."

Chapter 3
The Interrogation

I left the restaurant and stood outside on the pavement for a few minutes. The salubrious air helped me recollect my composure, and I walked to the top of the crossroads to hail a cab, luckily one was waiting unoccupied.

"Lovely day isn't it guv? Where we headin' today?"

"St Thomas' hospital, please."

"Okay, nothin' too serious I hope." I didn't reply.

My mind was continually replaying the incident, and I was trying to think how it could have occurred. If Mr Bertrand had an allergy, surely he would have known about it? Restaurants nowadays are meticulous with food labelling and preparation; I couldn't believe this could have been some kind of mistake. Maybe it wasn't an allergy and the EpiPen antidote was administered for no reason—it would explain why he remained unconscious. The different scenarios of how and why raced through my head. The taxi crossed Westminster Bridge and before I knew it we were at the hospital.

I entered through the Accident & Emergency entrance and walked up to the reception desk. "A friend of mine has been admitted to hospital and I'd like to see him please," I said.

"What's the name?"

"Alain Bertrand."

"Oh, he's in Hope Ward; you might not get entry though, it's a private wing."

"Thanks." After getting directions, I made my way.

Hospitals are buildings not many people like. Most are a sprawling warren of endless corridors with basic decor. It's quite amusing how attempts are made to spruce up interiors with the odd plant pot and painting; this one was no different. I found the ward and pressed the buzzer to enter.

"May I help you?" the duty nurse asked.

"Yes, I'm here to see a friend, Mr Bertrand."

"You may come into the ward but you'll have to ask the gentlemen outside the room if you can go inside." This perplexed me somewhat but the nurse pressed the buzzer to let me in.

Mr Bertrand was in the Red Room. As I approached it, I could see two men in suits outside with their backs to the door. They instantly shifted their glance at me.

"Is it possible to see Mr Bertrand?"

"Definitely not!" came a reply in a harsh French accent.

"And who may I ask are you?"

"We are not to allow anyone into the room. Mr Bertrand is now under the Embassy's guard."

I stood there in disbelief. What was going on, was his situation quite serious? "How is he?"

"I cannot give you any information."

"I was with him when he fell ill," I said.

"Only close family are allowed to visit," one of the guards said.

The door to the room had a window, but it was shielded. With the events that had occurred, I decided it was best to leave. "Thank you anyway." I turned around and left the ward. The hospital wasn't too far from my flat, and I began walking towards Lambeth Bridge to get to the north side of the River Thames. It would give me time to absorb what was going on.

As I crossed the bridge, I went past the spot where Nancy and I first met several years ago. We were both attending a boat party; an invite had come my way from my friend Andrea who couldn't attend, and Nancy just happened to be a friend of a friend. The venue was a steamboat departing from Lambeth Pier, and I was told to meet Andrea's friends on the bridge, rather than trying to find them at one of the numerous berths adjoining the riverfront.

My initial memory of Nancy was catching her looking across the river at the towering skyscrapers that make up the City of London. I recalled her beautiful face and softly spoken demeanour when we were introduced. We began talking straight away and remained entrenched in conversation all that evening. The boat left the pier and did a return trip to the Thames Barrier, with me pointing out landmarks along the way. I proposed to her last year, shortly after I had purchased the flat in Marsham Street. Reminiscing about the boat party afforded a minor break from my anguish. As I sluggishly crossed the bridge my phone rang, it was Stacey.

"Hello Josh, are you okay?"

"As well as can be under the circumstances."

"How is he?"

"I don't really know, I didn't get to see him, he's under some sort of protection."

"Well, that's strange; when I called the Embassy to say he wasn't going to attend the function I got the impression they already knew what had happened."

"Anyway, I won't be coming into the office for the rest of the afternoon."

"That's understandable. I also informed David Highfield and he's aware of the situation."

"Thanks, see you tomorrow."

I got to the top of the bridge and walked past a social housing estate run by the Canopy Foundation, it's where my cleaner Chela lived. She had recently emigrated from Argentina and formed a small community of Latin Americans who lived there. They were hard-working, decent individuals, several of whom had taken jobs in my apartment block.

Once past the estate, I could see Marsham Street straight ahead. *Nearly home*, I thought. A minute later, I was outside my apartment block, I went inside and straight to bed.

I must have been asleep for over an hour and was abruptly woken by Nancy. "Wake up, have you been drinking too much at lunch again!" she shrieked.

"What time is it?" I opened my eyes and it was still light outside. Nancy was sprawled over the bed examining me for clues as to why I was lying down in my suit.

"Time you got up!" she retorted.

"I came home early, and no, I haven't been drinking," I said.

"It's 5 o'clock. Why are you in bed?"

"I've had a very bad day. My client was taken to hospital, he had some sort of allergic reaction during lunch."

"Oh Josh, sorry to hear that, poor man," she said, finally calming down. "What exactly happened?"

I explained how the meeting had gone and the events at the restaurant. She was naturally shocked but surprised too that I wasn't allowed to see him. "He must be an important person," she said.

"It's the lack of news that's getting to me. All I want to know is that he's alright."

"Don't worry darling, I'm sure things will be fine in a few days. I'm going to pop downstairs to the gym and will be back to make dinner. You just rest now."

"Okay," I said as I buried my head under the covers again. I had no intention of going to sleep but desperately wanted to hide from reality. However, my attempt at remaining in bed failed when a loud motorbike with inadequate silencers began accelerating outside and the noise reverberated up the tall, close-quartered buildings, forcing me to get up. Nancy returned from the gym and made a modest supper of ready-made pasta. I began eating, but I was unable to strike up a conversation.

"It'll all be fine Josh, you're not to blame in this situation."

"I know, but the questions from the police seemed to imply some sort of guilt on my part."

"The best thing to do right now is to forget about it and go to work tomorrow and talk things over with your boss."

"I guess you're right."

"Hey, guess what?"

"What?" I said with a tone devoid of any interest.

"I saw the most perfect shoes for the big day as I was passing through Victoria Street."

"Good." This attempt at cheering me up wasn't going to work.

"There's a new boutique in Victoria Place, and they've got an introductory discount." I listened to her going on about the new shop and the range of shoes they had on offer. She continued, "I've still got loads of stuff to buy for the honeymoon. Oh, I'd love to go to the Bahamas one day." I reluctantly smiled, these types of hints weren't subtle I mused. A honeymoon to the Caribbean would be as expensive as it gets!

"You know, Sardinia and the Amalfi Coast have always appealed to me," I said. "The scenery is stunning and they're a short flight away." Now that got her thinking.

"Sardinia, I've heard such lovely things about it, and the *Costiera Amalfitana* sounds like such a romantic place."

Finishing my food rather hurriedly, I got up to put my dishes in the dishwasher.

"You haven't eaten much."

I was about to respond when the doorbell rang. I looked through the video intercom and a policeman was standing outside. My heart sank as I opened the door slowly.

"Mr Rosenburg?"

"Yes, that's me."

"I'm Detective Chief Inspector Hardcastle from New Scotland Yard. Can I come inside for a few moments?"

"Certainly."

"Who is it?" came a shout from Nancy.

"It's a policeman from Scotland Yard, he needs to go over a few things from earlier today," I replied. The policeman came inside and took a cursory glance at the hallway and the rooms leading off it that had their doors ajar. "We can go into the study," I suggested.

He followed me in and made himself comfortable on a brown chesterfield armchair. "Nice apartment," he said. "Let me introduce myself properly, I'm the Detective Chief Inspector investigating Mr Bertrand's case, you can call me Inspector Hardcastle, here's my card. I need to ask some additional questions as there have been some developments, I hope you understand?"

"Of course, how is Mr Bertrand?"

"I'm told he is in a very serious but stable condition," Inspector Hardcastle said. I felt relief that it wasn't the worst news I could have received, but it was nevertheless unsettling.

"Did he have some sort of food intolerance?" I asked.

"That's what I wanted to talk about. It appears that Mr Bertrand could have been poisoned."

"Poisoned!"

"Yes, poisoned, but we aren't sure," repeated the policeman. "It may not have been a random event. Mr Bertrand had an allergy to Brazil nuts. We found a high concentration of the active ingredient that causes the allergy in his bloodstream. He could have got it from contamination in his food, or someone may have put it there intentionally. We are still investigating and examining the kitchens at the restaurant."

"So you're saying it might not be an accident?"

"Yes, normally in these cases a mistake or oversight happens in the kitchen, but we can't rule out sabotage."

"Why would anyone want to do such a thing?"

"We don't know the motive at this stage, Mr Rosenburg, but I need all the information I can gather. I'd like to ask some questions."

"Go ahead."

"How many times did you see Mr Bertrand on his current business trip?"

"Only today."

"Can you go over in detail the events of the day?"

"Yes, of course, they've been playing in my mind over and over again." I started with greeting Mr Bertrand in reception and taking him over to the meeting room. Then I explained how the meeting had got underway.

"Did he eat or drink anything at the meeting?" interrupted the policeman.

"Yes, I believe he had a coffee and some biscuits. The kitchen attendant at Omega could tell you exactly which brand. But we have client files which detail dietary requirements for each meeting."

"Oh, did the kitchen attendant serve the drinks?"

"No, he normally pops into meetings and does all of that, but not this time."

"Wish we had one at the station. Carry on."

I began talking again and was stopped after a few minutes. "Did your client intake any food or tobacco that he had on his person?"

"No."

I continued my dialogue up to the point David Highfield had interrupted the meeting.

"Did David offer him another drink?"

"No, not in my meeting but you may want to speak to Miles about his one." I continued and relayed the drinks order I had placed at the restaurant bar. "Oh, I should mention someone recognised Mr Bertrand and approached him for a brief chat. Soon afterwards we sat down for lunch."

"Oh yes? Can you give a description of the person? Did you catch a name?"

"No, but he did introduce himself to Mr Bertrand. Maybe a Mr Jourdain? Or Janvier?" The inspector continued making notes without looking at me.

"Could this individual have spiked his drink?"

"Maybe so; or it might have been a distraction for someone else to do so," I suggested.

"True. We are going over the footage from CCTV, however, it was quite crowded in the restaurant yesterday and we couldn't get a clear picture of where you guys were at the bar. The shots of the table were much clearer but the only people in close proximity to Mr Bertrand were you and the waiter. I understand you were expecting a colleague to turn up, but he cancelled?"

"That's right. Miles was meant to join us but he got busy and to be fair to him, he did decline with adequate notice so as not to delay lunch."

"I see, tell me, did the waiter carry your drinks to the table?"

"Let me remember—no, we finished them at the bar. Then we ordered a bottle of water between us."

"No wine at the table?"

"No."

"Who opened the lid on the bottle? Was it the waiter?"

"Yes, I think so. You can appreciate I can't recall every small detail."

"Of course, try and cover as much as you can. Do you remember the waiter that was serving you?"

"Very clearly."

Inspector Hardcastle reached inside a pocket and produced a photograph.

"Is this the gentleman who was serving your table?"

The distinctive double chin and swept-back hair of the man in the photo was definitely the waiter. "Yes, that's him."

"Please continue."

I explained how efficient the service had been and Mr Bertrand's comment on the exquisite cuisine. Then I paused before mentioning the conversation about Drenchin' Doughnuts, which brought a smile to the inspector's face. When I began talking about Mr Bertrand falling ill, he seemed a bit disinterested, maybe because he had several accounts already from other people.

"I understand you tried to see him in hospital?"

"That's right, but he had some sort of embassy protection."

Nancy knocked on the door and popped her head into the room. "Can I get you a drink officer?"

"No thanks. Sorry to encroach on your evening, I'm just doing some routine questions."

"That's okay."

She left and the policeman resumed his questioning.

"Can you think of anyone else who had any contact with your client at the restaurant?"

"No, not really. I have given you all the information I know."

"Can you tell me how many times you had met Mr Bertrand and when and where?"

I thought for a few moments and then gave him some sporadic information as I recollected my previous business meetings.

"What was his relationship like with other individuals at your company?"

Again, I entered deep thought before giving patchy accounts of the dealings that Mr Bertrand had had with Miles, David and one of my ex-team members called Thomas. After I'd finished, he seemed fairly content with all that we'd covered.

"Thanks for answering my questions, I'll be off now."

"Sure, thanks." We got up, and I showed him to the door. As soon as it closed Nancy came out of the living room and gave me a big hug.

"He's only doing his job," she said.

"I know, it's the misfortune of being part of such a distressing situation and then the ignominy of facing all these questions. By the way, this is strictly confidential but—Mr Bertrand could have been poisoned. The police are still running tests."

"That can't be so!" she said. "Who would do such a thing?"

"I don't know, but many people knew him."

We sat down in the lounge, and I went over the discussion I'd had with the inspector.

"This is the last thing we want hanging over us leading up to the wedding," she said.

"Don't worry darling, I'm sure they won't need me anymore—I've told them all I can."

It was 11:00 p.m. when we finished talking and Nancy decided it was time to go to sleep. I was tired and emotionally drained, but not sleepy. How could the poisoning have happened? It must've had something to do with the man who interrupted us at the bar. Or maybe the chef was part of the plan? It was hard to work out what might have happened. My mind circled around until the only antidote was to shut my eyes and try to think of nothing. But that didn't work either. So I switched on Sky Sports. A Champions League game featuring Chelsea had just begun. They were slow to start and parts of the match remained rather dull. I turned to my iPad, searching for nut allergies and poisons. I needed to know how the poisoning may have happened. Could it have been a mistake?

When the final whistle sounded, Chelsea had convincingly beaten their opponents. The camera focused on the new manager, punching the air with joy. "At least someone is happy today," I thought and with that went to bed. The next morning, I got up quite early and breaking a habit of a lifetime, failed to look at my diary. I put on a grey suit and was ready at least half an hour before Nancy.

"What time are you getting in for?" she asked.

"Oh, I'm in no hurry. I'm sure it's going to be another day of questions."

"Good, I'll be ready shortly, we can leave together." I knew that meant fifteen minutes of wardrobe selection and multiple applications of hairspray, so I switched on the TV and waited.

When she was ready, we left the apartment. The concierge offered me an obligatory greeting, and I barely responded; today, I felt like keeping my head down. As we stepped outside, I noticed it was remarkably colder than yesterday. A blanket of clouds above reflected my sombre mood. Nancy and I walked hand in hand along Horseferry Road, not feeling the need to exchange words. But she was the first to break the silence.

"As I said yesterday Josh, all you can do is get on with your work. Your client is now in safe hands and I'm sure you've got other important meetings to deal with."

"That's a good point. I'm not sure what my agenda is today. The CEO has already emailed me not to say anything to anyone. No doubt he'll want a more detailed update."

"Oh, by the way, I haven't spoken to my father yet about the wedding car your friend Henry has offered," she said. "I'll get back to you today."

"That's fine," I said. Henry was the individual who had recommended investing in Drenchin' Doughnuts. We had met at university where we studied Economics together. He was a typical best friend, a good laugh, trustworthy, helpful, and sometimes very irritating! He lived in a Georgian townhouse overlooking Vincent Square, also in Victoria.

The conversation fell silent again, and we walked towards Strutton Ground, which held a market on most days. We squeezed through the market stalls which were pretty busy with early shoppers, and got to the place where we normally said goodbye. We hugged each other for a long time before departing to our respective places of work.

Passing through St James's Park I wondered what to tell my co-workers and what was best kept quiet. It wouldn't be fair to Mr Bertrand if every grim aspect of the event was relayed to outsiders when he was unconscious in a hospital bed. I decided not to say anything and only comment on a 'need to know' basis.

I entered the office building and went straight to see Stacey. She saw me approaching and got up. "Hi, Josh, how are you?"

"As well as can be under the circumstances."

"Don't worry, it'll all work out. By the way, David wants to see you first thing this morning."

"Okay."

"How's his condition now?" she whispered.

"I'm told he's stable." I didn't want to mention the evening visit by Inspector Hardcastle.

I went to my desk and everything appeared normal. Then it occurred to me that apart from Stacey and David everyone else was oblivious to what had happened anyway. I logged onto my PC and began scanning my emails, without really acknowledging the sales staff on the other side of the room. My first email was an invitation to another Investment Management meeting titled 'Investment Portfolios—Improving Accounting Methods'. However unexciting it sounded, I would have swapped yesterday's client meeting for it any day! I looked through the rest of my inbox and noticed Miles had sent me an email asking about lunch. I didn't reply. Moments later, the phone rang, it was David Highfield.

"Hello Josh, are you okay?"

"Yes, thanks."

"I'd like to see you in my office, please."

"I'll be there in a second."

I put the phone down and walked through reception.

David's office was next to the meeting room where I had met Mr Bertrand. I knocked on the door and he beckoned me to come in. His office was almost as large as the sales department. On the opposite side of the room was a sitting area with sofas and a coffee table. From there, one could see out of the large sash windows facing the front of the building, which provided a good vista of the activity on Pall Mall below. David's desk was to the right and bookcases filled the space to the left.

"Please take a seat."

I sat down and waited for David to start the conversation.

"I appreciate it was a difficult thing to witness what happened in the restaurant yesterday, and thanks for turning up today. How's your fiancée by the way?"

"She's well—it can be disconcerting when the police turn up to your apartment in the evening asking questions."

"Yes, I know, I was also questioned yesterday. The French Embassy has been in touch; Mr Bertrand is in a stable but serious condition."

"I see, no change from last night then?"

"Whilst the police are investigating this matter it should be treated with the utmost discretion. We do not want any publicity around this event."

"I totally agree," I said.

"The only people aware of the situation are the board members, Miles and Stacey, and I've already spoken to them."

"Understood."

"As far as you're concerned it's business as usual. If you have any questions, please contact me directly, even at home. You may carry on with your activities as normal and Josh, try not to think about things."

"Sure."

I left David's office feeling more at ease, particularly as it wasn't just me who had been subjected to a police enquiry. I got back to my desk and checked my diary; I had a full schedule with conference calls in the States just after lunch. I took heed of David's advice and thought it was best to get on with my day job, and began preparing for my conference calls.

Chapter 4
The Investigation Begins

It was close to noon, and I was still sitting at my desk when the phone rang.

"Hi, Henry," I said.

"Hi Josh. How are you today?" came a jolly voice, practically beaming down the line.

"Fine," I said, tersely.

"You sound a bit distant, everything okay?"

"Yes, it's fine."

"Worrying about your portfolio again? Well, an investigation into Drenchin' Doughnuts has begun regarding the lawsuit. Tests are centred on the mocha filled with raspberry…shame that was one of my favourites!"

"I'm not interested in that right now!"

"Fair enough…I was just giving you the low down. Hey, did you see the Champions League's knock-out stage last night, Chelsea did well."

"Yes, I watched parts of the game. Anyway, Henry I need to go, see you later."

"You don't sound like yourself. If anything's up, let me know."

"I'll chat to you later, take care," I said putting the receiver down without properly hearing Henry say goodbye.

I resumed my work, and it wasn't long before lunch came around. Grabbing a sandwich from one of the coffee shops on Piccadilly was an easy choice, so I walked to the lifts and pressed the button to descend. As I stood there waiting, my mind turned to yesterday's meeting, maybe I should explore the room in which it was held? I approached the room and looked through the door's peephole. It was empty and I sneaked inside.

Events from the meeting raced through my mind, and I felt the tension come back through my body. I recollected that Mr Bertrand had eaten some chocolate digestives. I went to the sideboard and opened the cabinet. Inside were stacked all sorts of biscuits.

I found the packet I was looking for and inspected the ingredients. The traditional recipe for digestives eschews nuts of any sort, and this packet was no different. Then I read a disclaimer beneath the ingredients saying the biscuits were made on a production line that may handle nuts. But the policeman had said the concentration of allergen was so strong it couldn't have come from trace elements. It seemed highly improbable that any poisoning could have occurred in the meeting. That got me thinking further. Who could have known about the allergy? Surely it'd be on the client's personal file, as all in-house caterers had access to clients' dietary requirements. Instead of popping out to lunch, I went straight back to my desk.

I logged onto my computer and went to the client services directory in the file system. After entering the secure password, I could see several scanned files in Mr Bertrand's directory, and I organised them by date. Picking the oldest one, I opened it on screen, conscious of anyone walking past my desk.

The document was the original client services agreement signed between Omega and Mr Bertrand, dated 4 September 1993. Mr Bertrand's initial investment of 30 million dollars was stated, a paltry sum compared to his current investment. I skimmed through the twenty-odd pages and found no reference to client dietary requirements. The second file was a revised client agreement with much the same information.

I continued looking and got to the fourth file, this one was five years later than the first. It detailed the client's address, phone number, interests, business dealings and dietary data. The handwritten entry clearly spelt out the allergy to Brazil nuts. I hadn't noticed the time and glancing at my watch, I had 45 minutes to fetch some food before my next conference call. I locked my computer and headed for the lift again.

The nearest café to my office was hardly my first choice when it came to culinary excellence, but in time-starved situations, it helped. As I stepped outside onto Pall Mall, the spring air seemed fresh and I took in a few deep breaths. Cutting through several side streets, I made my way towards Piccadilly, passing antique dealers and fine art boutiques along the way. When I saw Waterstones bookstore, a thought occurred to me.

I entered through the rear door on Jermyn Street. It was relatively busy with lunchtime shoppers, and I made my way to the second floor, going straight to the biology section.

Let's see, I thought, *I've got to be quick.* The problem was there was so much choice. At least six shelves were dedicated to all sorts of adverse conditions and allergic reactions. Where do I begin? I glanced down the aisle and looked blankly at the rows and rows of books.

A few university students were also eyeing up the same shelves as me. *Maybe I could ask them for some input,* I thought. As I was about to do so, a man in the distance entered my aisle and then turned around again. I caught a glimpse of his face, it was familiar. Side-tracked, I stepped towards him so that I could clearly see his side profile.

That's the man, I thought. That's him, the one who approached Mr Bertrand the other day. What should I do? I had to speak to this man, even if it meant missing lunch or a meeting. I walked closer to him, gathering my thoughts as to what to say. Should I mention what happened at the restaurant? Maybe this guy was a stone-cold assassin? What could I lose, I was in a public place, nothing was going to happen to me here. So I decided to confront him.

As I walked towards him, he decided to leave for the stairs. I didn't want to raise the alarm that I was following, so I ensured a reasonable distance was maintained between us but increased my pace. The man appeared to be in a hurry and striking up a simple conversation whilst in pursuit now seemed difficult. However, I followed him down the stairs, and he had made his way past the queue for the tills. As I got to the revolving doors he had already left the building and turned right.

Before I was able to exit, several people entered the revolving door from the street. I could only wait patiently, and then I made a dash for it. On the street now, the man was at least fifty metres ahead. So I decided to run.

"Hey," I shouted. A few pedestrians turned around, but my target kept on walking.

"Hey!" I shouted again, this time close enough for him to swivel and stop, bemused that I was running towards him.

"Hi there," I said. "Sorry to interrupt you."

"Hi," replied the man. "Can I help?"

"I believe we met yesterday," I said.

He looked at me briefly. "I don't think so."

"Yes, you were in the Golden Orchid yesterday—we have a mutual friend, a Mr Bertrand?"

"Ahh...yes now I remember, you assisted me with directions. How can I help?"

I thought I'd introduce myself in the hope of eliciting his name. "I'm Josh Rosenburg, one of Mr Bertrand's long-standing friends. You are?"

The man paused before answering. "I'm Daniel Joubert. How can I help you?"

"Did you know Mr Bertrand fell ill yesterday at the restaurant?" I was looking for any sign that might give this man away, something in his reaction or what he might have to say.

"Oh, gosh," came a genuinely surprised reply. "Is he ok?"

"It seems he had an allergic reaction of some kind."

"That's terrible," said Mr Joubert, still displaying his concern. "When I spoke to Mr Bertrand, he appeared in fine health."

"Yes," I said, "but during the meal, he was taken ill. They had to call an ambulance."

"This is terrible. I don't particularly know him, except for seeing him a few times at investor events. I hope your friend makes a full recovery, really sorry about the news. I've got to go now."

I didn't get any opportunity to probe him any further with my questions. But his concern and demeanour appeared normal. My gut feeling told me this man had nothing to do with the poisoning. Surely the police would follow him up anyway from the CCTV?

Slightly dejected I glanced at my watch. I had already missed the beginning of my next meeting. Maybe I should go and see the head waiter of the Golden Orchid? Yes, at least that might help me piece it all together again. The Golden Orchid was open as usual, nothing gave away the unfortunate incident from a day earlier. There was a queue for the tables and I joined it, waiting patiently. Sven was directing people, and slowly, I crept forward in the line. Then a flashback entered my head. The food inspector had been in front of us, maybe he would have seen what went on in the kitchen. This was something I urgently needed to raise with Sven. Eventually, he turned to me.

"Hello, Mr Rosenburg," he said with a sullen tone.

"Hi Sven. I'd like to talk to you."

"Sure," he said. "How is your friend?"

"Not so well I'm afraid."

Sven called a colleague to take over his duties and took me to the bar.

"It's shocking," said Sven. "In all my time I've never seen someone react like that!"

"I know, awful to witness," I replied. "Have the police been here today?"

"Yes, this morning for further questions. We had to close for evening service yesterday. They were taking all sorts of tests and examining the camera footage."

"Any guesses as to what happened?"

"Not really, you know all the kitchen staff are shocked. It's beyond them. They pride themselves on the cleanliness of the kitchen. We are super conscious of allergens and keep nuts, wheat and dairy under strict control."

"What about the food inspector?" I enquired. "I overheard he was inspecting the kitchen, maybe he saw something?"

"Oh, yes, the guy from the Food Inspections Agency. He gave his statement to the police too. He could only complement our kitchen hygiene."

"Was it an impromptu inspection?"

"No, we had the meeting in the diary a few days ago—not that we needed to change anything in the kitchen."

"Can you do me a favour—do you have his details?"

"He gave me a card, but I'm not supposed to do anything like that."

"Sven, you've got to help, for your restaurant and my client's sake. He's lying in a hospital bed."

"Okay, but we are all being scrutinised, especially the chefs and waiters, so you need to be careful." Out of Sven's pocket emerged a business card. I took a photo of it on my phone and said thank you, then left.

I headed back to the office, although it was 3 o'clock by the time I got there. My ability to do anything constructive at work had diminished. My new focus was on the inspector; could there have been something untoward in the kitchen? But how could someone possibly have targeted my client? The timing would need to be spot on. One would need to place a poison at the correct time on the correct dish being sent to the table. It would have been too difficult to schedule to that perfection.

At my desk, I pondered over a few theories on the poisoning idea. Maybe I should give the Food Inspections Agency a call, just to check things out for myself. Maybe my private research could help Inspector Hardcastle in some way? Or maybe not! Following that chap in the bookshop proved unfruitful and quite out of my character. I was getting desperate.

The business card of the food inspector listed a landline and mobile number; I decided to call the former to check its validity and verify the details.

"Hello, Food Inspections Agency, can I help you?"

"Hi there, I would like to speak to one of your inspectors, please?"

There was a pause. "Sorry, we don't give details of our inspectors. As you can appreciate, we need to keep utmost discretion around restaurant visits and who's running an inspection."

"I do see that, the thing is I need to check something."

"Sorry sir, let me re-iterate; we do not give any details of our inspectors. A restaurant owner should not know in advance which person will be visiting them. We only give them two days' notice that an inspection has been scheduled."

"I get your point," I replied.

"Thank you. Goodbye."

Time to try the mobile number. I called it, and it went to voicemail instantly without any greeting.

Great, I thought, *another lead that's turning out to be a dead end.* If the inspector was responsible in some manner, there was no way he'd have known I'd booked a table at that precise time and day. Was there another mastermind behind the whole operation?

I decided to leave work early and on the way out, coincidently shared the lift with the IT director.

"Hi, how was your day?" he asked.

"I've had better. Yours?"

"Great, I've been going through the results of the email phishing exercise I conducted. Do you recall that bogus email about winning Wimbledon tickets that everyone received? It was me running a test for the Compliance department!" He appeared proud of himself and seemed like the sort of guy who revelled in bad news. "Guess how many people fell for it—at least 15, some of them quite senior," he laughed. "They'll need to redo their security training!"

"Phew," I said, "it almost caught me out!"

"Anyway, see you tomorrow."

Walking through St James's Park, the day's events went through my mind again, but the conversation in the lift resonated with me. I needed a strategy to get hold of Mr Cuthbert-Jones, maybe I should conduct a phishing exercise of my own? Needless to say, it couldn't be executed from my work computer. Opening the front door of my apartment I was greeted by Nancy. She gave me a big hug. "Why don't you forget about work now? I've made you a lovely roast dinner."

"That sounds great. But I do need to do some research afterwards."

"Oh I see, I understand there's a lot to take in right now. How was everyone at work?"

"They were good, it was pretty much business as normal," I said, shamefully thinking about how I had chased down Mr Joubert.

"Well, at least let's have our dinner in peace."

The roast was welcome comfort food on a day like today. Shortly after eating, Nancy and I sat down to watch another episode of the Netflix drama we'd started the week before.

"Darling, I need to do some work now, I'll be in the study."

"Sure. You can have a guess what I'll be looking at!" she said with a smirk. "By the way, the Chelsea manager's children have started at my school. Poor darlings, one of them was teased a lot today."

"I'm sure they'll retaliate soon if their dad is anything to go by!"

"Yes, I was thinking how could I stop the other children from being so mean."

"A promise of football tickets is always a carrot on a stick. It works with my clients!"

"Hmm...good idea, Josh."

I went to the study and my focus turned to the plan to contact the food inspector. I decided I'd send a phishing email pretending to be the manager from Golden Orchid, in the hope of getting a response. Do you know how easy it is to send an email from a bogus account? In my case, the email domain name would be changed from *@goldenorchidrestaurant.co.uk* to a fabricated *@goldenorchidrestaurant.com*. Hopefully, Mr Cuthbert-Jones, if he even existed, might not notice and respond! The recipient was the general contact email provided on the Food Inspections Agency website. The email read:

Dear Mr Cuthbert-Jones,

It was a delight to welcome you to the Golden Orchid on Monday. Your courteous manner towards the kitchen staff was appreciated, and they would be glad to assist you again with your inspection. As you may be aware, there was an unfortunate incident at the restaurant that evening and in haste, it appears you left your wallet behind.

Please reply to this email with a suitable time the restaurant staff can return your item along with a short verification of your ID.

Yours Sincerely,
Sven
Head Waiter

The guilt of sending the email was overpowered by the thought of my dear client being poisoned. All I had to do was monitor the bogus email address for any replies, assuming someone might fall for my ruse. For the remainder of the evening, Nancy and I continued watching Netflix, interspersed with me taking short breaks to check the bogus email address. No reply came through.

It was Wednesday morning. I arrived at work and for breakfast opened a pot of porridge I'd bought on the way. Before I could take a mouthful, the phone rang. It was David Highfield.

"Hi David."

"Hi Josh, have you got a moment?"

"How long will it take please? I'm having a quick breakfast and then I've got a client call at 10 o'clock."

"I see. Finish your breakfast and can you get Katrin to cover for you instead?"

There was no need to knock on David's door as it was ajar in expectation of my arrival. As I entered and closed it behind me, I noticed another man in a suit sitting beside David. It was the police officer who had been in my flat.

"Please take a seat, Josh," instructed David. "I believe you know Inspector Hardcastle."

"Yes indeed, we had a lengthy conversation."

"There have been some developments and the inspector needs to speak to you."

"Mr Bertrand's case is now being treated as attempted murder," declared the inspector. "We believe there was intent to poison him, and it failed. We have eliminated all suspects in the kitchen and waiting staff at the restaurant. Having spoken to the prime suspects, I'm afraid you are the key figure in this and therefore I need to go over more questions."

"I told you all I know on Monday," I proclaimed.

"I appreciate that sir, but I need you to accompany me to the station for further investigation."

"I haven't done anything," I said, turning to David.

David then spoke. "Josh, the police need to carry out their investigation. I cannot have you in the office whilst this is ongoing. It's not good for you or the company. Therefore I am suspending you from your duties until this has been resolved."

"What! David, I don't know how I've been caught up in this situation, but I'm totally and utterly innocent," I pleaded.

"The police need to do their job. Mr Bertrand is lying in a hospital bed; you need to go through this."

Mr Hardcastle interrupted. "Mr Rosenburg, I'd like you to come with me now to the station. There is an unmarked police car waiting outside."

"I need your company pass, Josh. You may not enter this building or contact anyone connected to the business, which means both your co-workers and clients. Also, your computer account will be locked so you can't log in from home. Do you understand?"

I looked down and shook my head in disbelief.

"Do you understand, Josh?"

"Yes. What are you going to tell everyone?"

"We'll say you're dealing with a personal matter. You need to say the same if anyone tries to call you."

I abruptly stood up, gave the policeman an angry grimace and slapped my company pass on the polished desk where we were sitting.

The inspector got up, and I quietly followed him out. We departed the building, an unmarked car with a driver and front passenger were waiting outside. Inspector Hardcastle opened the door and I sat down, paying little attention to the other occupants. The car left, and we headed for the station.

Chapter 5
Chelsea Police Station

I'd never set foot inside a police station before and didn't know what to expect. Would I be pushed into an interrogation room and harassed? For all I knew, I might be spending the night in a cell with a double murderer! The horrendous turn of events had completely confounded me.

The police car turned into King's Road, Chelsea, and I glanced outside the window. It was lunchtime by now and there were droves of shoppers milling in and out of the designer shops and boutiques like ants around a nest. Rambling tourists, not paying much attention to shopping were observing and pointing at places of interest. The alfresco cafés were busy and traffic on the road fairly pedestrian. While people were going about their normal business, I was being detained for attempted murder. It was absolutely ludicrous!

"Are we almost there?" I asked.

"Only two minutes away," replied Inspector Hardcastle. The driver started indicating right and we turned off King's Road down a side street. Another right and I could see the station. It was a 1930s building, purpose-built as a station. Numerous police vehicles were parked outside and the driver stopped at the entrance.

"Here we are," announced the inspector as he got out. The driver and front passenger remained in the car as I also stepped outside. The inspector entered the station first and held the front door open for me, I entered apprehensively.

The interior was no different from the front desk of a doctor's surgery. Plastic chairs around a cheap-looking table formed a seating area and a receptionist stood behind a tall desk. The walls were covered with message boards, to which leaflets were pinned highlighting crime prevention methods. Beyond the reception area, I saw a dishevelled man being escorted by two muscular officers in uniform. I was now in the same category as these unpleasant characters. We walked straight through reception and I was guided into a room labelled 'Interview Room 5'.

"Please take a seat," said Inspector Hardcastle. "Can I get you a drink?"

"No thanks, just tell me what you want from me and how long it'll take."

"You have been brought here to assist with the investigation of the attempted murder of Mr Alain Bertrand. I cannot give you an estimated duration for the interview sir. We will now be joined by Sergeant Clarke who will conduct the interview alongside me."

"Am I under arrest?"

"You have been brought here for questioning; no charge has been made at this point."

I waited several minutes in a prickly silence. The door opened and a short, well-built lady entered the room. She did not smile, nor seemed capable of doing so. She sat down and placed a digital recorder on the desk. As I looked at the device I noticed her hands were quite feminine and appeared to have been transplanted from a more slender creature.

"Good afternoon, Mr Rosenburg; my name is Sergeant Clarke. The purpose of this interview is to capture the facts regarding your dealings with Mr Bertrand. Do you understand?" she said while pulling out a notepad.

"Haven't I done that already?"

"We need to build a complete picture from our side. This conversation will be recorded for later use. May I request that you answer all questions truthfully and to the best of your knowledge."

I didn't say anything, and she carried on.

"Further to the responses you gave to Mr Hardcastle yesterday, I'd like to go over some of the events again."

She began by asking precisely the same questions that were covered the previous day. I did not bother complaining and candidly explained the events as I had recalled them.

"Do you know how much Mr Bertrand has invested in your company?" she asked curiously.

"I was looking at it the other day—approximately $250 million, actually it was $270 million six months ago but his portfolio has fallen recently!"

"Did you know he featured in France's equivalent of 'The Times Rich List' last year?"

"No, but then a handful of our clients are probably on those lists."

"So do you have any idea what he may be worth in total?"

"Well, someone with that kind of portfolio size…let me see…probably around the $500 million mark."

"Which of his personal dealings outside of your company were you familiar with?"

"Only what I read in the papers and any information he shared with me."

"Please elaborate, Mr Rosenburg."

"Umm…he recently failed to acquire Spacey, the music retailer. I know he's a major shareholder in Vendome Jean Industrials. He made his name by founding an aeronautical engineering firm, but the name escapes me."

"Are you aware of any other clients in your company that had contact with Mr Bertrand?" she said.

"I'm not aware of them personally, but the answer is probably yes. Sometimes clients are introduced through existing investors. I heard that in the early days of Omega, Mr Bertrand introduced several acquaintances from continental Europe, obviously in return for lower account charges. I don't know who they were or whether they're still invested in the firm. I should add that the company holds client events several times a year. Anyone dealing with the firm is welcome to attend and there is an opportunity for investors to mingle with one another. Given that he'd been with us pretty much from the beginning, he may well have had contact with other clients."

"How much commission do you earn from running his account?"

"That depends; my remuneration is tied to overall company profits. Understandably a large proportion is based on personal performance, and that for me means generating fee income from my client base."

"You haven't fully answered the question."

"It's difficult to quantify. Where's this leading anyway?"

"Okay, let me put it another way. If you were to lose Mr Bertrand's account, how would that affect you financially?"

"In such a case, I'd get a low bonus, even nothing at all."

"Did you think that was a possibility prior to the meeting yesterday?"

"Well, it always crosses one's mind, especially when investment returns are bad."

Sergeant Clarke then paused and looked at her notepad. It was Inspector Hardcastle's turn to resume the onslaught of questions.

"Nice place you've got there in Westminster—how long have you lived there?"

"I moved there about a year ago."

"We did a credit check on you and your finances, it's routine procedure of course."

"Fair enough, do you have some sort of point to make? I'm failing to see your line of questioning."

"Pretty hefty mortgage you've got—I don't envy you," said Inspector Hardcastle with a wry smile. "Our checks also revealed you've lost a fair bit of money on your investments."

I was taken aback by the amount of investigation they'd conducted into my affairs. "Yes, but who hasn't?"

Sergeant Clarke then interjected, "We've seen a big rise in financial crime, particularly since the recession. You know rational, normal people take silly risks when faced with money problems."

"What are you trying to insinuate?" I said angrily. "Are you saying I tried to commit some type of fraud?" The pair remained silent and instead were gauging my reaction and interpreting my body language. "Well, it's crazy to make such a suggestion. This interview is moving into the realms of science fiction!"

"Calm down, Mr Rosenburg," said Sergeant Clarke. "At this stage, we're only fact-finding. By the way, were you aware of Mr Bertrand's allergy?" I froze at this question. "Maybe yesterday morning you did some digging around on the computer system?"

"Well, yes actually," I said uncomfortably. "Following the revelation about him being poisoned, I thought I'd check his client file. In a document dated ten or eleven years ago, it highlighted his allergy."

"Who else has access to the file?"

"My team definitely, I'm not sure about other people."

"A scan of Omega's computer systems hasn't revealed any wrongdoing yet. Do you have client information stored at home on a laptop or PC?"

"No, I had remote access to the computer system at work but that has been revoked."

"Who else in your team had contact with Mr Bertrand?"

"Over the years quite a few people. But recently, it's been me, Miles and David. Oh and Thomas who no longer works for Omega."

"Are you surprised someone tried to kill him?"

"I'm stunned. I can't believe it's happened to him."

The questions stopped and silence ensued. Both officers were busy taking notes and I looked despondently around the interview room. Sergeant Clarke stopped scribbling and looked up with a stare that consumed my entire being. For the first time since yesterday, I felt fear, real fear, fear that something horrible was going to happen.

My mobile rang, and out of reflex I went to answer it but stopped.

"May I?" I asked.

"Go ahead," she said.

"Hello."

"Hi Josh, it's me!" said Henry. "Hey, guess what? You're in luck, the bailed-out bank stocks that you hold have finally announced a profit! What a momentous occasion, they're going up at last!"

"I'm really busy right now, I'll call you back."

I put the phone down, and Sergeant Clarke was still holding her stare.

"The inspector and I need to talk—we're going to leave you here for ten minutes. Would you like a drink?"

I felt exasperated; my mind was in disarray; and I was devoid of any emotion. "A glass of water please," I said.

After passing me a glass, I was left alone to contemplate my fate. What could they do? Where was the evidence? What was my motive?

Ten minutes later they re-entered the room and sat down. Sergeant Clarke breathed in deeply and spoke in a low voice. "Mr Rosenburg, based on the evidence that we have gathered and the information you have provided, you need to remain at home until further notice. The police force requires more information to make a formal arrest but for now, there is an injunction against you and you must remain at home."

"This is going too far!" I shrieked. "I did not try and kill him, do you understand?" My fear had turned to anger. I couldn't comprehend the logic with which they had formulated such a conclusion.

"Please remain calm!" said Inspector Hardcastle.

"How about the other suspects? What about the chap that approached us at the bar or the chef at the Golden Orchid?" I exclaimed. "It could be anyone from the kitchen."

"No, the staff were all examined for traces of the poison, on their hands, clothes and kitchen worktops, but nothing. It wasn't the regular staff members."

"The man at the bar, his name was Daniel Joubert. Have you checked him out?" I said guiltily, knowing I had chased after him on a London street.

"We are examining all video evidence, it appears you gave him directions. Do you know the man at all?"

"Certainly not," I said, attempting to hide a quivering voice. "What about the food inspector? Do you know there was a kitchen inspection going on at the time?"

"How do you know?"

"Because the food inspector arrived just before I did, and I overheard his conversation with the head waiter."

"We interviewed him at the restaurant and checked his credentials with the Food Inspections Agency, he is one of their employees. He had booked the inspection well in advance of your arrival, so we believe he is all above board. I suggest you go home and seek legal advice. You must remain at home except for essential shopping and medical appointments. Please report to the station tomorrow morning at noon. Any breach of the instructions may result in you being electronically tagged or arrested."

I didn't say a word. I left the room without acknowledging anyone. I walked straight out of the station and caught a taxi home.

When Nancy returned from work, I explained the turn of events. "Unbelievable," she said. "Unbelievable, just utterly…" The phone rang, it was Henry again.

"Hi Josh, how are you?"

"Okay." I felt it was time to have a chat with him about things. "Henry I can't speak now but do you fancy meeting up tomorrow? I've got to speak to you about something."

"I knew something was up," he said gleefully as if he had a sixth sense. "Where, at your place?" Then a thought struck me; if they'd been monitoring my computer at work, maybe my calls were being recorded too.

"I'll call you back," I said.

There was way too much to think about. The interview questions kept racing around in my mind as I tried to make some sense of what was going on. It was unfathomable they were now trying to concoct a motive to seal my fate.

The comment regarding them scanning Omega's computer systems made me wonder how thorough they'd been. If someone had wanted to kill Mr Bertrand, the motive was surely money. I could understand the line of questioning geared towards financial crime.

Then I had a wild idea—why not interrogate the computer systems myself, to see if there had been any suspicious transactions? But I couldn't do this alone—I needed someone at the company with access to the entire file system. There was only one person in the IT infrastructure team that I trusted and who had the requisite technical proficiency. Whether he'd jeopardise his career to help me out was another matter.

"Nancy, may I borrow your phone?"

"Why?"

"I'll explain later, give me the phone please! I have to make an important call; will be popping downstairs for a bit."

I went into the external corridor and found an enclosed area by the fire exit. I needed to call Hitesh, a long-standing member of the IT department and its most knowledgeable member. I rang his mobile and luckily he picked up the phone.

"Hello, Hitesh," I said.

"Hello?"

"It's me, Josh. Are you still at work?"

"As it happens yes. The email server decided to die just before I was about to leave for home! It's always a case of bad timing."

"Ah, I see. Look, I need to talk to you about something. It's highly confidential, and I don't want to get you in trouble. You can't be seen talking to me."

"Is everything ok? How can I help?"

"I'm in a hazardous situation. There's some fraud occurring on a client's account, and they think it's me."

"That sounds serious."

"It's very serious," I whispered, nervously looking up and down the corridor. "I need you to have a look at the backup tapes and some confidential files on the system. Could you do that for me please? I totally understand if you don't want to, but I'm in deep trouble and completely innocent."

"I'm willing to help to a certain degree, but if I get caught you know I could lose my job, or worse!"

"I know, but I swear I'm innocent. The police have scanned Omega's computer system and found nothing."

"That's probably what crashed the email server! They couldn't find their way around the system if I gave them my password," Hitesh quipped.

"Are you willing to help me?"

"Of course Josh—you've always stuck up for me, and you helped me with my last promotion! If anyone does ask questions, I'll blind them with technical mumbo-jumbo."

"Good. Can you examine every transaction on Mr Bertrand's account going back to inception? That's potentially 16 years of stored tapes. I need to know if there was any connection to other clients or members of staff, or if any transactions looked strange. It's a tall order, but I know you can do it."

"I definitely can. Now that my evening is written-off anyway, I'll write a program that can do most of it automatically. It'll have to run overnight—there's a lot of data to access."

"That'd be great. Could you call me on this number tomorrow morning?"

"Sure, depending on what time I get to bed. Glad you mentioned the police computer scan—I thought we'd had an attempted hack from Asia again."

"I'll repay you for this. I've got to go now but let's chat tomorrow."

My suspicion was that maybe there had been some spurious payments to offshore accounts, which could point the finger of blame away from me. After sending Henry a short message about meeting at Drenchin' Doughnuts tomorrow morning, I walked back into my apartment.

"Would you mind swapping phones for a while? Mine might be bugged," I said softly.

"Yes, you can take mine temporarily. I'll use my spare SIM card in your handset," Nancy said. "By the way, I'm tired and have an early start tomorrow. Are you going to bed too?"

"No, not yet. I need to do a little more thinking..."

Chapter 6
Meeting at Drenchin' Doughnuts

The next morning, hit by the reality of being dismissed from work, I got up relatively late. Nancy was already leaving the apartment, and I had just started making coffee. It was 8:30 a.m. now, and I was constantly checking my phone to see if Hitesh had left a message, as well as monitoring the bogus email account for a reply from the Food Inspections Agency. Nothing had come through from either source, and I kept checking whilst watching a breakfast chat show.

Donning a pair of jeans, a smart jacket, comfortable loafers and baseball cap, I duly left my apartment at 10 o'clock to meet Henry. Downstairs in the foyer, the concierge gave me the standard acknowledgement while taking a fleeting glance at my attire. I turned into Horseferry Road and arrived at Drenchin' Doughnuts less than a minute later.

The shop stood out because of its luminous frontage, it looked clean and comparatively upmarket. At this time of the morning, most of the customers were people rushing to work. Hardly anyone was eating at the tables, so it was quite easy to spot Henry reading his paper.

As I approached, he saw me and got up.

"Do you want to get yourself something? I'd stay away from the Raspberry Mocha!" he chuckled, referring to the health and safety investigation.

"Yes, I will, back in a second," I said.

I went up to the counter and looked at the menu on the blackboard. It included a lemon and lime doughnut infused with marinated pumpkin seeds, a vanilla one with tarragon sprinkles and a chocolate flavour with coriander leaf; the Raspberry Mocha was unavailable.

Behind the counter on the back wall was a coffee serving station and shelves with gift items. The neat display of gifts was separated by an open door leading to the kitchen. It was a shame this creative doughnut place had not launched properly with such a distinctive product line.

"Would you like a doughnut, sir?" the shop assistant asked.

"No, only a coffee please," I said with some disappointment as I digested the sum of money I'd invested in this place.

I collected my drink and sat down next to Henry, who began asking questions straight away. I covered the entire story from the initial meeting on Monday to yesterday at the police station, obviously leaving out the part concerning Hitesh. Throughout my recollection of the events Henry looked bewildered but interested; this was as exciting as it got.

"You're basically under house arrest," he said. "Damn—it's serious! If someone is after his money, the best way to get it would be using a cover—identity fraud is big business nowadays."

"True."

"With basic documentation, someone can pose as another person and make all sorts of transactions."

I was thinking along the same lines as Henry. "Can you give me an example of how that might happen?" I said, half knowing the answer.

"Well, identity fraud involves someone pretending to be somebody else, by obtaining their personal details online or manufacturing fake documents. Once this is done, the fraudster makes transactions using the bogus identity. Most of these transactions are eventually spotted by banks and government agencies, but the fraud is committed in such a short time frame that it's often too late for the authorities to pursue any useful leads. I think you need to find out what was happening on Mr Bertrand's account, but I can see how you're the prime suspect."

"Thanks for your support!" I said sarcastically. At least he had cemented my viewpoint on the situation. My phone rang. "Please excuse me for a second," I said.

"Hi Josh, it's Hitesh. I've found something that looks highly suspicious! I can't discuss it over the phone—we need to meet up."

"Okay, when?"

"As soon as possible. It looks like someone is covering their tracks and the information I have might be lost."

"I'll call you back in ten minutes," I said and put the phone down. I looked at my watch and got a fright—it was 11:55 a.m.! I was going to be late reporting to the police station.

"Oh, damn!"

"Everything ok?"

"Yes," I said trying to regain my composure and thinking about what to do next. "It looks like there's some suspicious activity on my client's account," I whispered to Henry.

"I told you so," he said. "You need to do your own investigation—it appears the police don't have the same level of insight as you to judge what's going on."

"You're right Henry, you're right," I repeated with a sense of urgency.

"Hey Josh—don't turn around but there's a policeman hanging outside."

"Oh no," I said. "Is he looking inside?"

"He's peeking at you intermittently."

"Oh, great! I need to speak to Hitesh."

"Who?"

"Can you do me a favour? I'm going to leave now, can you distract the policeman?"

"How?" asked Henry.

"I don't know. I need to see Hitesh."

"Who is Hitesh?" he asked again.

"Look, I'm going to leave, just do something to get that man to stop looking at me," I said.

I got up and facing straight down, walked swiftly towards the entrance of the restaurant, keeping the corner of my eye on the policeman outside, who was wearing a luminous yellow jacket. As I opened the door to get out, he blocked my path. I stared at him for a few seconds and then my natural instincts took over. I swiftly turned around and ran towards the counter.

The policeman started to chase me and putting one arm on the counter I leapt straight over. As I ran into the kitchen I heard a loud crash as the policeman collided with Henry, who was attempting to get up. *Well done, Henry!* I thought.

Taking a fleeting glance behind me, I clumsily collided with one of the chefs. The chef yelled something incomprehensible and then looked at the policeman, pointing in my direction. The large kitchen had three aisles separated by shelves of cooking utensils, with several cauldrons of doughnut mixture to one side. As I ran past one of the cauldrons, my hand smashed into several plastic bowls on a shelf.

Doughnut ingredients fell into a cooking pot that was slowly being mixed. By this time, the policeman had got to his feet and resumed the chase. After dodging several other kitchen staff, I ran back down one of the aisles with the arm of the law following suit. I whizzed past the cooking pots again and as I did so, out of reflex action I picked up the two bowls I had dropped.

The policeman froze for a second assuming that I was going to use them as missiles. But I just threw them to one side and resumed my getaway. All the staff had run into the seating area by this point, and I could see the back door of the kitchen. I dived through it into an outdoor space which was a delivery area.

I now had a couple of choices, follow the delivery road back to the front of the restaurant or jump over a wall that led to a car parking area behind the Canopy housing estate. Given the plump appearance of the policeman and his rather slow reflexes, I thought scaling the wall was a good option. With a run-up that I had not practised since triple jump training at school, I managed to leap and hold on to the top of the wall. Within seconds, I was over it and running through the car park. The PC was still struggling to overcome the wall, and I quickly ran down a pathway between two buildings, moving out of sight.

Meanwhile, at the restaurant, Henry was still talking to customers and enjoying being the centre of attention as people questioned him about what had happened.

"He didn't look like a dodgy person," said a lady who'd been standing by the counter.

"No, he's not!" said Henry. "It's a case of mistaken identity and my friend is completely innocent."

"What's he accused of?" asked another.

"I don't know, you'd need to ask the policeman," Henry retorted.

The kitchen staff returned to their duties and one of the chefs began inspecting a bowl of ingredients that had fallen into the doughnut mixture. He suspiciously looked at it, dipped a finger into the mixture and licked it.

"Hmm…red onion and mustard, interesting flavour," he muttered and with a nod of approval walked away.

What am I doing? I thought. *This is crazy!* Maybe the policeman had nothing to do with monitoring me, and it was my paranoia that caused him to give chase. My mind was not thinking straight. I had just run away from a member of the law—this was serious stuff!

An energetic sprint around one of the buildings led me onto Page Street, moments from my block. I was conscious that I still had an appointment at Chelsea police station. *Damn!* I thought. *I need to phone Hitesh—what should I do?* Speaking to Hitesh was the most important thing, he had information that could get me out of this mess.

I ran from Page Street into Regency Street and saw the policeman heading the wrong way. I immediately slowed down and took off my jacket and cap in an attempt not to get recognised.

Right, I thought, *speak to Hitesh and then attend the police station.* My apartment was yards away, but I wasn't sure whether to go in. I decided not to. Instead, I began walking towards the river; it'd be quiet down there, and I could gather my thoughts.

I reached the riverside and my demeanour was far calmer. I sat down on a wooden bench and looked out across the Thames. The cruise boats ferrying tourists were leisurely drifting by and the bridges were full of slow traffic. The sky had a grey hue which was reflected in the muddy water of the Thames. I called Hitesh.

"Bear with me one second," said Hitesh. He was probably finding a suitable place to talk as I could hear walking and the slamming of doors. "Now, I've found something highly strange on Mr Bertrand's account and also another client account."

"What is it?"

"Well, it's quite bizarre. There are some very dubious financial transactions on both client accounts, but not recently—not even last year, but five years ago."

"Five years ago!" I exclaimed. "How can that be related to what happened to Mr Bertrand yesterday?"

“I need to meet you as I can’t make sense of the accounts—I’m not a client relationship manager and don’t understand the ledger entries. By the way, have you heard of a client called Mr Charles Bonham? He’s English but with a French passport.”

“Never heard the name,” I said.

“Damn. I searched for his name on the internet and nothing. He does have an active account with us. We have his personal details and mobile number on file.”

“How’s this related to Mr Bertrand?”

“Well, looking at Mr Bonham’s account, around five years ago, a large sum of money was lent to Mr Bertrand. Does that sound strange to you?”

“No, some of our clients are business acquaintances and do lend money to each other on joint business ventures.”

“Since the transaction, there hasn’t been any entry or dealings on Mr Bonham’s account. He has a relatively small balance of one million Euros left in cash, no stocks or bonds.”

“Hmm, maybe he started banking with another institution? Who knows?”

“Where can I meet you, Josh? I can’t cover all this on the phone.”

“Green Park. Can you come down during your lunch break?”

“Definitely. I’ll see you at 1:00 p.m.,” confirmed Hitesh.

I knew I’d be in serious trouble with the police for showing up late at the station, but first I had to look at what Hitesh had found.

Chapter 7
Revelation in Green Park

I exited the ticket barriers at Green Park station having caught the Piccadilly line from Pimlico. As I climbed the final steps of the station ascending to street level, I could see the pavement was heaving with people and given I was now on the run, I felt safety in numbers. Trying not to glance at anyone and keeping my head down, I made my way towards the park's entrance. Once inside, a quick scan of the immediate vicinity told me Hitesh hadn't arrived.

I sat down on a bench and waited. The daffodils were in blossom and this was unquestionably the best time of year to visit. Green Park, with its wooded meadow and no lake, had a simplicity and serenity, providing a calming welcome from the frenetic ordeal that I'd just been through. It was 1:10 p.m. and still no sign of Hitesh. The phone rang, the caller display showed 'Christine'. Then I remembered I still had Nancy's phone and chose to terminate the call.

I'd been waiting another five minutes before I saw Hitesh enter the park. He paused for a second and picking me out sitting on the bench, walked towards me.

"Boy, I'm glad to see you," I said. "I'm in a lot of trouble."

"I can't believe the police can be barking up the wrong tree so badly—who's running the investigation, Inspector Clouseau?" replied Hitesh. "By the way, I've downloaded most of the data on my laptop."

"Can you explain more about the dealings on that other chap's account—Charles Bonham, wasn't it?"

"Yes. Mr Bonham seems to be an acquaintance of Mr Bertrand, they opened their investment accounts with the firm at roughly the same time." He paused, looked around, and then continued. "Mr Bonham lent Mr Bertrand approximately 20 million Euros in a loan agreement, similar to an IOU, five years ago. The repayment of the money with interest is due this coming Monday, according to the copy of the agreement on both clients' files. The interest has been set at 4 million, to be paid back with principal."

I looked at the loan documents on screen and after a few minutes asserted they were bonafide. The 20 million loan must have been paid to and from accounts not managed by Omega. However, the repayment to Mr Bonham was due from Mr Bertrand's investment account; the account that I managed.

"This could be easily resolved if we could get hold of Mr Bertrand, but he's incapacitated. From what I can see, a sum of 24 million must be paid out on Monday at noon. It has all been signed and sealed with the correct legal paperwork."

"So, my question is; will Mr Bertrand have enough to cover it?"

"Yes. The Payments team who monitor daily cash flows would have flagged this up anyway. Let's think for a second. Let's assume this IOU was fraudulent in some way—then Mr Bertrand would definitely question such a sizeable chunk of his hard-earned cash being transferred elsewhere. If the money were transferred on Monday and then redirected to an offshore account on the same day, then his Daily Investment Statement for transactions on Monday wouldn't be published until Tuesday morning. The earliest he would catch a glimpse of his money transfers would be Tuesday, one day too late to do anything. And that's assuming he even checks the statement promptly."

"So it seems for the fraud to work seamlessly the money needs to be transferred elsewhere as soon as it arrives in Mr Bonham's account," said Hitesh. "It all needs to happen on Monday, before any detection the following day."

"Yes, that's right."

"But why do you suspect the loan arrangement is suspicious?"

"It simply doesn't sound right. Thinking about it, a man of Mr Bertrand's wealth would not need a loan from a friend. It's something he would have mentioned too, and I've been looking after his business for almost a decade. Was 20 million even deposited in Mr Bertrand's account? Maybe it was and all is good, but on the other hand, we have no proof whether it was paid. The key thing is the repayment is to be made via Omega's payment system to the account specified in the agreement. The 24 million will leave the account which I manage on Monday at noon."

"So, let's go over the facts again just to get it in my head. Someone has created a loan agreement, and we have a record on both clients' files. We see a scheduled payment due on Monday, at noon. The repayment was entered into our system 5 years ago, at the outset of the loan agreement. The initial loan of 20 million was made outside of Omega's jurisdiction, so we have no evidence if it was real or not. If it was, then Mr Bertrand would have no reason to question it. If it were false, he would be none the wiser, as there would have been no money transfer anyway?"

"That's right," I said. "And clients' files are only available to authorised staff who manage them in confidence. Someone with the correct authority could have produced the loan agreement and planted copies of it in both clients' files. The same person could then have instructed the Payments team to schedule the repayment, there's no way they would doubt it if the correct paperwork was produced by an authorised staff member."

"And the repayment of 24 million is live and ready to be processed on the settlement date—it's a legal obligation."

"We need to get hold of Mr Bonham. Let me take his details. God forbid, but if Mr Bertrand dies, how would anyone question the loan?"

"True—if one member passes away, the written, binding contract is all that anyone can go on I guess?"

"Where is this money due to be paid?" I asked.

"In the Champs-Élysées branch of Credit Union de Paris. I've got all the details on this memory stick. When would Mr Bonham withdraw the money?"

"Any thief would want the money moved as soon as possible. I wouldn't be surprised if there are instructions already at Credit Union de Paris to move the money on Monday to an offshore account."

Hitesh promptly shut his computer and wished me good luck before setting off. I knew the risk he had taken in seeing me and I was grateful. It was 2:00 p.m. by now, and I felt a pang of hunger. More importantly, I had missed the appointment at the police station. Should I bother going? Maybe I'd get electronically tagged or placed under arrest? I decided not to go; it was way too risky. Should I call instead? I reluctantly headed in the direction of my apartment but prepared myself for another one hundred metre dash in case a policeman caught sight of me.

Walking back, I had time to hypothesise about the fraud and how it could be uncovered. There was no point in trying to prove what happened to the initial 20 million Euros given to Mr Bertrand, assuming it even happened. My hunch was that it was never paid, merely a bogus IOU to legitimise the repayment five years later. This would make the second part of the transaction more believable.

Getting rid of Mr Bertrand when the repayment was due was the perfect scenario to stop anyone questioning it. The only way to stop the transaction was to intercept it. But as Hitesh said, it was scheduled at the Champs-Élysées branch of Credit Union de Paris.

I was certain a further instruction had already been given to launder it into an offshore account, that's the instruction I had to intercept, but it could only be given by Mr Bonham. Any new instruction or changes to an existing instruction would require the authorised account holder to visit the branch and show all their relevant ID. It wasn't a small sum of money—any bank would require validation in person.

As I exited the park, my mind was fragmented with numerous trails of thought. How would I tell Nancy what happened today? Was it worth going to the police with what little evidence I had? Should I continue my investigation, no matter what the risks?

That's it, I decided. I had to go to France. I had to get to the bank and stop the transfer of money.

Amongst the plethora of open questions, one had to be answered relatively quickly. How would I get to France whilst being under house arrest?

Chapter 8
The Plan

I was peering left and right every ten seconds or so as I made my way towards the main road that leads to Regency Street, which ran parallel to the road where I lived. I weaved through the side roads heading towards my apartment. When I was within viewing distance of my block, my heart began racing, and I automatically started looking for the policeman from whom I had run away earlier. The road was fairly empty, I approached the entrance and hurriedly went in.

"Good afternoon Sidney," I said to the porter. "Has anyone been in asking for me?"

"No sir, I've been on duty since this morning and no one. Should I be expecting anyone?"

"Not really, see you later," I said.

I gathered the coast was clear for now. The corridor was empty, and I walked up to my front door and peered through the peephole, which wasn't much help other than it told me no one else was peeping from inside. I opened the door with the stealth of a ninja and tried to gauge any signs of unwanted presence inside. The apartment looked as it should, there were no strange sounds or odours. I went inside and examined each room, no one else was present.

I sat down in the study. Again I thought about the incident at Drenchin' Doughnuts and that maybe, just maybe, it was my paranoia that had led the policeman to chase me. I needed to think about my next move. I decided I should call the police station, but only after I'd inspected the memory stick Hitesh had given me.

I inserted it into my laptop and began analysing the personal files of Mr Bertrand and Mr Bonham. Mr Bonham had registered an address change to the Cayman Islands about five years ago—a coincidence? Probably not. He was a

French citizen and since his relocation hadn't made any transactions in that time, but this was no reason to preclude him from having an 'active' status at Omega.

Clients with inactivity of ten years or more on their accounts were normally given 'orphan' status. An orphan fund is one where the owner's whereabouts are unknown, and their money is safeguarded until someone makes a claim on it—normally beneficiaries in a will. I was slightly surprised Mr Bertrand had never mentioned Mr Bonham.

Looking at the files again I could see that the last meeting Mr Bonham had at the Pall Mall office was over six years ago. He had met Steve Chatsworth, a client services manager no longer at the firm. I concluded there was no point in trying to ascertain who else might have known him.

The data on the memory stick breached virtually all directives of the Data Protection Act; I had copies of driving licences, account passwords and personal addresses. Mr Bonham's Omega account had a balance of €1.1 million at the Champs-Élysées account that Omega managed. Then something that Henry had said sprang to my mind, "Identity fraud is big business. Imposters pretending to be someone else can make withdrawals on their accounts, given they have the right documentation."

If Mr Bonham (or whoever the fraudster was) had perpetrated this crime and tried to land me in the slammer, maybe it was time I served him a lesson. Maybe I could pretend to be him and withdraw the €24 million before he could get his greedy hands on it. How could I do such a thing? It might be easier than I thought—I had all the necessary information electronically that I needed, but not the paper identification. Where could I get it made?

Suddenly, I heard a key being inserted into the front door and I froze. The door opened, and I peered through the gap in the study door to see Chela enter the apartment.

"Josh, what are you doing here?"

"Oh, today I'm working from home," I said casually, trying to sound unperturbed and normal.

"Josh, I need to speak to you. A policeman was asking about you earlier."

"He was here?"

"Yes, he was asking all sorts of questions, and then he went away, and I went to the dry cleaners."

I knew the porter had lied to me.

"How long ago was this?"

"Oh, about two hours ago. Is everything okay?"

"Not quite, Chela," I confessed.

"What's the matter?"

"I'm sort of accused of trying to poison a client at a lunch meeting," I explained.

Chela looked baffled. "What are you going to do?"

"I'm not sure, but I may need to get away for a while."

"Does Nancy know?"

"Yes she does, but no, not about the getting away part," I added.

"Where are you going to go?"

"I need to get to Paris, but obviously I can't travel as myself, I'll be arrested. I need to pretend to be someone else."

"How are you going to do that?"

"Chela, I wonder if you can help me. I'm wondering if you've heard about anyone on the estate that has, or knows of, people that have got into the country illegally."

"This kind of stuff is not right, Josh! I know one cleaner working here that got into the country unofficially, but I don't approve. What are you going to do, go to Paris, and then what? Get stuck there! You are sounding crazy, Josh!"

"I know Chela, but I'm desperate here. Please, you need to help me."

"Promise me one thing. Did you have anything to do with the fraud?"

"Absolutely not! It's a big mix up and the idiots at the police station have no clue. I need to do some investigation myself—the police don't know much about this sort of crime as I do. I'm trying to help them. Instead, they're wasting their time monitoring me."

Chela nodded. "Alright," she said. "You want to speak to Eliza, the housemaid on the fifth floor. You go up there now. Don't mention my name."

"Thank you so much, Chela," I said. "Please don't tell Nancy. I'll give her a call later."

I had made up my mind. I was going to become Mr Bonham himself and go to Paris. Second-guessing the criminal's next move was the only way to stop the fraud from taking place.

I hastily got changed, then, pausing for a moment, reached underneath the bed where Nancy and I kept a safe deposit box. There we stored cash for emergencies as well as our passports. I opened it and snatched the £4,000 it contained, as well as my passport. Finally, clutching my laptop, I left the apartment not knowing when I'd return. On the fifth floor, I began searching for Eliza, which was easy; I discreetly followed the sound of a vacuum cleaner to the open front door of apartment 51.

"Eliza?" I asked.

A short, round lady turned to me and then switched off her cleaning device.

"Yes, how can I help?"

"I need your assistance, I know you can get a…a passport."

She looked startled. "How do you know?" she asked.

"Look, I need some help. I have to get to France, but the problem is I require a false passport, so I can travel as someone else. I need one made, you know, unofficially. I understand you know where I can get one?"

"I might do. You the one with the beautiful wife?"

"Well, she's my fiancée. We're getting married next month." I replied.

"Chela has mentioned you. She says you're kind and nice."

Thank God, I thought. "So, who are these people? I need to speak to them."

"Look, they are dangerous. I don't really know them. I helped them once or twice to deliver some passports, I needed the money, plus I owed them for bringing me into this country. But I stopped, I was afraid. Chela told me it was wrong."

"You can trust me. Tell me please?" I said pulling out my wallet. "Does this seem okay?" I handed her what must have been £1000. Reacting very calmly she took the money and stashed it away in her apron.

"Listen, what I tell you is a secret. Don't tell anyone you spoke to me, you promise?"

"Yes, certainly, I swear I won't mention it," I said.

"You need to go to the corner flat in Block D on the estate. It's got a blue door, next to the refuse area. I don't know the number, but it's right in the corner on the ground floor. But they are dangerous."

"I'm not going to try anything silly. Thank you."

As I walked past the porter I gave him a piercing look. He sheepishly stared back at me, probably visualising me handcuffed and being dragged by the scruff of my neck.

It wasn't long before I was outside the Canopy housing estate again. I got to Block C and then turning off Page Street I could see the signs for Block D. The small tenements were looking worse for wear. Some had cracked windows, others torn curtains and the courtyards overgrown with moss.

At the turn of the last century, these buildings were the pride of Westminster, cheap social housing that was built to last; after all, they had survived both wars. Some of the ground floor kitchen windows were open, and the aromas reminded me of Chela's cooking. I was thankful she had given me such a useful lead.

I arrived at the right block and saw the refuse area straight away. At this stage, my heart was racing. It was the craziest thing I had done to date. Next to the refuse bins was the apartment Eliza had described.

Chapter 9
Going Undercover

I knocked on the blue door, but there was no response. I knocked again and still no answer. I then moved to the window and gave it a slight tap. The door opened slowly, but with the security chain engaged. A strange chemical-like smell crept out of the flat, and I took a step back.

"What do you want?" came a man's voice from behind the door. Only one of his hands was visible.

"Hi, I was told to come here, I need a passport," I said.

"Who sent you?"

"Someone who works in my apartment block."

"What is their name?"

"I promised not to say."

"Do you have any ID?"

"Yes. I have my driving licence and passport."

"Give me both of them," demanded the man, who had now stuck his hand outside.

I reached inside my pocket and hesitantly handed over the items. The door closed, and I was left standing outside, wondering if I'd ever get my ID back.

After a minute, I heard the security chain being unlocked and the door opened. A European man wearing a hoodie and dark glasses stood in a dimly lit but warm corridor and gestured to me to come inside. I was taken to a small room at the back, with a square wooden table with several laptops on it. A display cabinet piled with papers was leaning against one wall and the window was screened with decrepit plastic blinds.

"Take a seat, Mr Rosenburg," said the man; he had a strong Germanic accent. He left the room, and I waited for several minutes. I could hear two men speaking in a Baltic language; he reappeared, together with a short man.

"So you'd like a passport?" said the short man.

"Er, yes. I'm in a spot of bother, and I need another identity. It's just a temporary thing," I said with a degree of nonchalance.

"So, who do you want to be?" he asked with a smirk on his face. "I can't do Tom Cruise, he was taken this morning." His accomplice laughed.

"I've got a memory stick with the identity of a Mr Bonham. I need a passport, but a driving licence would also be good."

"You want a driving licence as well, it'll be a lot extra. Show me the stick," demanded the short man.

I handed the stick over, conscious that these men still had my ID. The man inserted it into a laptop and pointed to the screen.

"Which file do I need to look at?" he asked. I showed him the right one, and he brought it up on the screen. He then reached to another laptop and began entering some information that was shielded from me.

"Your friend Mr Bonham appears to be in hiding. He has travelled around quite a bit in his life, but not much in the last five years."

Hearing this information again did not surprise me. I assumed these men had hacked into government agencies. "Is he dead?" I asked.

He tapped away on the computer again. "Maybe, no one knows," came a slow reply. "He came to England and fell off the radar."

"Can you give me his identity papers?"

"In theory, yes, for the right price."

"How much do you want?"

"A passport is eight thousand pounds and a driving licence is five thousand pounds. But I recommend to you what I call 'The Identity Kit'. The Identity Kit is all you need in this world to start afresh, to build a new life. Many peoples have solved their life problems with The Identity Kit. Marriages have been saved, family reunions made possible, retirement dreams—"

"I get the idea!"

"It's ten thousand pounds and you get both documents; do you want it or not?"

"Ten thousand—there's no way I can withdraw that in cash in such a hurry."

"Don't worry, you can pay by card. Your payment will show up as a debit from an online jewellery store. It won't be traced."

"Is there any room for negotiation?"

"Do you work in sales?"

"Yes."

"Do you think a man on the run is in a negotiating position?"

"Who's looking for me?" I asked.

He reached inside his pocket and gave me back my passport and licence. "These are worthless, and I wouldn't use them unless you like prison food. I found a restriction on your passport with the UK Border Agency. If you try and leave, you'll be arrested straight away."

I nodded. "Ten thousand it is. I've got my debit card." I decided from now on I'd only use cash, especially if I got to Paris.

"Well, if you don't mind waiting, I need to use my printer," he said, as he got up.

I sat in the dark, warm and ink-smelling dining room, a world away from normality yet moments from my pleasant, bourgeois life on Marsham Street. What would I do once I became Mr Bonham? Was his disappearance just a convenience until the money arrived in his account? My mind was busy trying to hatch a plan together. I could try and withdraw a small amount from Mr Bonham's account and see if it worked, as a trial for the big sum. Then I'd hand over the money to the French police and tell them about the loan arrangement with Mr Bertrand. The plan seemed shaky and fraught with risk, but it was a way of proving my innocence. Getting to Paris wouldn't be too troublesome—the Eurostar train was now departing regularly from Kings Cross station, and it was only a short tube ride away.

The man who had opened the front door came back into the room. He handed me my memory stick and the new documents, which I inspected thoroughly.

"Very good," I complimented. "I also need printouts of this loan agreement."

"I'll do that for free," said the short man, dryly. He went to the printer room again and returned promptly, passing me the newly printed agreements. "In case you don't know, your old identity has been registered on Interpol too. Never forget; I am not your friend. You don't know us, and we don't know you. Any word of this meeting to the authorities, there will be worse consequences than prison." The short man opened a drawer from one of the filing cabinets, and I saw a gun. "Do I make myself clear?"

"Yes."

He closed the drawer. "You may go now."

I left the flat and heard the blue door close behind me. I was on my own now, but glad to have left that dank and dismal place. Should I call Nancy? I wasn't sure, but I should call the police station.

Looking up the number of Chelsea Police Station, I rang the general number.

"Chelsea Police Station, how can I help you?"

"Hi, my name is Josh Rosenburg, I was meant to report to Inspector Hardcastle at 12 but was feeling ill."

"One moment sir." After a couple of minutes, the sergeant with whom I'd had the interview interrupted.

"Mr Rosenburg, it is a criminal offence not to report to the police station on time under your circumstances. Being ill is no excuse. When are you coming in? Otherwise, we will be forced to arrest you."

"I'm sorry, I had a temperature this morning and felt nauseous. I'm heading there right away."

"Bye," replied the sergeant angrily.

I made my way to the Pimlico tube station with no intention of going to the police, not quite yet.

It was late in the afternoon and Nancy entered our apartment. Chela was there to greet her.

"Nancy, I need to tell you something. I spoke to Josh earlier, and I know he's in trouble."

"Oh, he told you," she said somewhat embarrassed. "It's absolutely ridiculous, can't believe the police have got it so wrong."

"Yes, but he seemed quite scared, I think he's planning to run away."

"Run away, huh, not Josh, he's got nothing to be afraid of," said Nancy, "he's not a murderer, and he wouldn't try and kill his most favoured client and the hand that feeds him! How else is he going to get me to the Bahamas!" Nancy shook her head from side to side.

"He was talking about getting a fake passport, you know, pretending to be someone else."

Nancy let out a laugh. "Who's he going to be, James Bond?"

Chela giggled but knew it was far more serious than Nancy imagined.

"Don't you worry Chela, he sometimes gets all panicky. I'll call him shortly."

"How was school?" Chela asked attempting to change the subject.

"Oh, I had such a productive day. You know the football manager on the top floor, one of his children is in my class. He was getting picked on because of his strong Latin accent. So I ran a class about European countries and languages. At the end of the lesson, he was teaching the kids how to speak in his native tongue. At least he's made some friends!"

"That's a nice story," said Chela. "I bet having a famous dad also helped!"

"Oh, he's a very popular boy now!"

"By the way, I've got to go," said Chela as she packed away her cleaning materials. "But please keep a close eye on Josh, he's not himself."

Chapter 10
Off to Paris!

Taking the tube to King's Cross was the best way of staying anonymous; a taxi was out of the question. Once on the train, I began counting down the five stops to my destination. Before it had reached Warren Street, the penultimate station, I noticed a man looking at me in an unnerving fashion. It was a face I didn't recognise.

Maybe getting off at the correct station might give too big a clue as to my intent to travel abroad. I decided to leave at Warren Street. As I suspected, the man also got off. *Damn,* I thought, *I've got another chase on my hands.*

At street level, I began walking down Tottenham Court Rd. The man followed, with some difficulty as he tried to remain out of view, but I kept turning around constantly on guard. A large group of tourists walking slightly ahead of me made the perfect decoy. I got in amongst them and then darted into a furniture store. The man following went straight past. Sensing the need to be extra cautious, I went up the escalator to the first floor, deciding to hang around for five or so minutes before continuing my journey.

Could it have been a plain-clothed officer? It was conceivable I had been followed to or from the Canopy block of flats. There was no time to lose. Being followed by the law was now a given; I had breached the terms of my house arrest, and they were clearly after me.

From the furniture store, I decided to jump on a bus, as there was only one stop to go. I wasn't in a particular rush to board a specific train, I only wanted to end up in Paris, preferably in one piece! From there, I could hatch the next stage of the plan; pretend to be Mr Bonham and arrange a meeting at Credit Union de Paris.

I got to Kings Cross and viewed the departure board, there was a train leaving in 55 minutes. Before queuing up at the ticket office, I needed to exchange some

Pound Sterling for Euros. A sense of excitement and fear gripped me simultaneously; it was the first chance to use my new identity. I waited for the queue to die down and then joined it.

"Can I help you, sir?" asked the cashier.

"Yes please, I'd like to change £2,000 for Euros."

"May I see your passport?"

"Yes, certainly." I handed it over hesitantly.

The cashier took no more than three seconds to look at the passport. "That's fine. How would you like your money, in 50 Euro notes?"

"Yes thanks," I said. I paid for the notes in cash and then walked towards the ticket office. It seemed all too simple. The ticket attendant looked at me and I requested an 'economy open return' without looking at the other ticket options on offer.

"Can I see your passport, please?"

"Of course," I replied, and handed it across with an air of confidence this time.

The attendant nodded. "The next train leaves in 45 minutes—do you want to board that one?"

"That'd be great." The ticket cost £195 and after purchasing it I went straight to the departure gate. My passport was checked once again and my ticket twice; that was all it took to board the train as an imposter. Luckily the seat next to me was empty, but an elderly couple were sitting opposite. The train departed on time. It wasn't long after my phone rang. It was Nancy.

"Hi, Josh!"

"Hi darling. How are you?"

"Where are you? It seems noisy in the background," she asked.

"I'm a bit busy at the moment, but I'm fine."

"How was the meeting at the police station?"

I paused. "It was as expected."

"When are you going to be home?"

"I'm not sure darling—they may keep me at the station this evening. There's a lot to get through."

"Is everything okay? What are those announcements I can hear in the background?"

"Oh, I'm currently walking through Victoria Plaza shopping centre." The couple opposite made eye contact with me at this comment, and I turned my head away.

"Are you on your way home?"

"Er, no I need to go back to work. Darling, I must go. I love you."

The conversation ended in haste, and I began thinking about my next move. Surely I'd need to fake Mr Bonham's signature if I had any hope of withdrawing his money. Now was a good time to put in a bit of practice.

The train had been travelling for about half an hour when an announcement was made on the tannoy.

"Can a Mr Rosenburg please report to the first carriage?"

I didn't hear it fully the first time around but then the repeated message was very clear. "Can Mr Rosenburg report to the first carriage or make himself known to a member of staff?"

The nature of the request was perplexing, as I now was Mr Charles Bonham! How many Rosenburgs could there be on the train? I decided it was time not to take any risks and felt the need to hide in the toilet or somewhere solitary. I got up and with my laptop satchel over my shoulder began walking towards the last carriage. Again my heart started racing.

Behind me, a guard was making his way through each carriage. I must have crossed three carriages, conscious of not arousing suspicion. The next carriage had a long narrow corridor and doors on either side labelled luggage. *Not a bad place to hide,* I thought.

I tried to open the nearest door, but it was locked. I then tried the next one along but it also didn't open. However, the third one opened easily and I made my way inside. Luggage was stacked on all sides, and at first, I couldn't see where I could hide.

Then I thought about moving some of the suitcases and replacing them in front of me. I heaved four or five cases and made a small pocket of space in the corner of the carriage. I then painstakingly put them back so I was completely hidden. The tannoy announced we were entering the tunnel; then I heard the request for Mr Rosenburg once more.

Surely I was the only Rosenburg with something to hide, and only I had a reason not to identify myself? Whoever made the request was after me. If it was the police, presumably they'd have sent an inspector?

The train entered the tunnel and all went quiet for a while. The silence was hard to fill and I began to hum very quietly; it was a way of de-stressing and filling the lonely space I was in.

"Can you stop that silly noise?" I instantly stopped. "You're going to get us caught!"

"Sorry," I said, not knowing to whom I was talking. Judging from the accent, he sounded French.

"What are you doing here? Who are you?"

"I'm looking for a bit of peace and quiet," I said.

"Very funny. I bet you're in the same boat—or train, should I say—like me," said the voice. "On the run, hey?"

I didn't say anything.

"Look mister, you might as well say something, there's a long way to go and we're both sitting next to stacked suitcases rather than people for a reason. I'll start—I'm Jon Krasinski, and I'm emigrating from England."

"You don't sound English. I mean, your accent is French," I said.

"Well, I am British according to my passport!"

"You attained British citizenship?" I asked.

"Er not quite. I got a British passport from a bunch of guys I know."

"I take it the bunch of guys didn't work for the immigration service?"

"No, I don't think they worked for anyone if I'm honest. But my life as a UK citizen is over."

"Got caught by immigration control?"

"Certainly not; a man of my skills is too smart to get caught," he said. "I decided to leave England of my own accord."

"Why?"

"As the famous Jim Rangers said a few weeks ago in The Daily Metro newspaper—the UK economy is finished!"

I was flabbergasted by his comment. He was referring to the legendary hedge fund manager Jim Rangers, a man everyone in the industry looked up to. I couldn't believe he was quoting an excerpt from one of his interviews. "The UK is not finished! It's temporarily going through a bad patch."

"Well, I think it's finished. But it's cool—I've become Italian now. Their economy is projected to come out of recession a lot quicker."

"Does your loyalty to a country depend on how well it's doing?"

"You're getting to know me well," the voice said, amused.

"Well, the United Kingdom may not be doing well at the moment but we'll make a comeback. We always have done."

"It's finished, my friend. There's nothing left. Unemployment is high, the budget deficit is growing, the pound is falling like a stone…"

"It's not all about money," I said. "We're a fair and tolerant society."

There was a pause.

"You're right my friend, you're right. The British were friendly and welcoming. I had a good time in the UK. I stayed in Liverpool cleaning windows for a while. Those Liverpudlians are a humorous bunch, very loyal to their football team. Who do you support?"

It struck me that this was one of the weirdest conversations I'd ever had, sandwiched between suitcases, pretending to be someone else and talking to a fellow I neither had met before nor could see!

"I'm not that keen on football," I replied. "Rugby is more my thing. Why did you give up window cleaning?"

"Oh, a friend of mine convinced me to join a car washing business in London, but it all went wrong. Having a sparkling car is not top of the list when a recession hits and you've lost your job. A lot of my customers were from the City, they would drive by on the way home in their Porches and Ferraris. But a lot of them lost their jobs and their cars, and the ones that kept their cars were happy to drive around with muddy alloys!"

"Sorry to hear that."

"One thing is for sure—I was given more help and support here than my native country ever provided me."

"So what did you do to make ends meet when the car wash business went under?" I asked.

"I distributed The Daily Metro outside Tower Hill station. The manager who got me the job knew I didn't have the right paperwork, but he could see I was desperate. It didn't pay much, but what a fantastic location. The whole area has such rich history; at lunch, I used to walk along the cobbled roads and the pier. What about you? Are you emigrating too? I can tell you were born and bred in England."

"That's right, I've lived in London all my life. I'm kind of emigrating temporarily," I said. Before I could continue, the tannoy system interrupted me.

"This is the last call for Mr Rosenburg. Please make yourself known to a member of staff. There is someone in the first carriage who needs to speak to you urgently."

The voice from the rack above hummed thoughtfully. "Hmm, can't be the police," he said. "You'd be arrested by now. Mr Rosenburg, I take it?"

"That's a good point," I said. If it wasn't the police, then someone else was onto me—probably Mr Bertrand's assassin. All at once, I had a new worry. There was more than the police to avoid.

The conversation fell silent for a long time, and then the tannoy sounded again. "Ladies and Gentlemen, we have now entered France. We hope you continue to enjoy your journey, and we should be at Gard de Nord on time."

Further silence ensued until I couldn't stand it any longer. "How are you going to exit the train?" I asked.

"Ah, I've done it many times. I wait until the train's passengers have almost departed, and then I get changed into a uniformed guard's outfit and escape down a service elevator. What about you?"

"I'm not so sure at this point," I said.

"Why are you hiding?"

I deliberated for a second, but then thought I might as well tell this guy what was going on. "People on the train are looking for me. But not as my new identity—but the one I left behind in England."

"I see."

"Do you think it'll be safe for me to go through border control with my new passport?"

"I don't know—I wouldn't risk it. But if you have a French passport, I can help you my friend, because I like you. When I depart the train wearing my uniform, I'll hold onto you. You must pretend you are ill. I'll take you with me through the staff entrance. If anyone asks, you are a consultant for Eurostar. If they ask to see your passport, just flash it at them. There is a different security clearance for staff and contractors. Trust me they won't ask questions."

The train must have been halfway between the Channel and Paris. I was beginning to feel cramp in my limbs but dared not risk getting up or even using the toilets. My stowaway friend had nodded off, and his incessant snoring was far worse than my humming had been. My phone rang, luckily I had lowered its call volume.

"Hello," I whispered.

"Hi Josh, that was a pretty good hundred-yard dash!" Henry said. "Where are you now?"

"It's a bit difficult to talk right now."

"Did you find out any more about the case? I'm telling you, it's identity fraud."

"You don't know how right you are, Henry," I said.

"I thought I'd call to see if you were okay—did you make your police appointment in time?"

"Kind of…"

"Oh, good. By the way, your portfolio's faring much better today. Some of the bailed-out banks have reported profits—can you believe it? They're actually making money after being close to annihilation only months ago. What a turn of events!"

"That's good to hear," I said in a lacklustre tone. "Henry, I've got to go now, but if Nancy phones, tell her I'm fine. Goodbye."

The stowaway woke up. "That nap was good," he declared. "I'm hungry, would you like some food? I have some spare."

What a kind offer! I thought. If this man wanted to, he could have alerted someone to my presence. He needn't have offered to take me through the staff entrance either.

"That's very kind of you, but no thanks. It's my turn to catch some sleep now."

The next announcement on the tannoy woke me up. "Ladies and Gentlemen, we are 15 minutes away from our destination. Please prepare for your departure."

"Damn! I need to get changed." I heard shuffling followed by someone leaping to the floor. I saw a thin small man with brown hair and stubble. He began rummaging through his backpack and produced a guard's uniform. Placing a name badge on his lapel, he heaped his belongings back into the bag. The badge read 'Javier Signoret'.

"Javier, shall I come out now?"

"Very funny," he said. "Let me find you that contractor pass—I'll be back. But please wait in here until the train stops. Someone will come in to pick up the suitcases, so remember to act ill."

"The way I'm feeling the acting won't be necessary," I said as I sprang to my feet.

The train finally stopped and passengers began to disembark. The time was 7 o'clock, and I stood up next to the stowaway. He opened the door of the luggage area and we both went outside. He seemed to know where he was going as he led me towards an area where other members of staff were congregating.

"Have your passport ready in case we get asked."

I was looking down and began leaning on my accomplice. There was a guard checking ID at the entrance to the service elevator. As we approached him we were stopped.

"Can I see your IDs, please?"

My accomplice replied in French with a fluency I rarely heard in the office from the European Sales team. He sounded authentic, and mentioned something about me suffering from travel sickness.

The guard then turned to me and I showed him my passport without flinching. We were let through, finally entering the station concourse. I had arrived in Paris.

Javier smiled at me. "You are free to leave my friend. Thanks for the company."

This man's story had not fallen on deaf ears. The small insight into his life showed me how privileged I was. This man had struggled to make ends meet in England and had thrown in the towel. But he had a positive outlook and jovial manner. I may not have agreed with his views, but he had repaid me the kind of generosity he had received in England and as a gesture of gratitude, I took off my Rolex watch and handed it to him.

"Please sir, there is no need. This looks very expensive."

"It is! Please take it, you have helped me very much," I said.

He nodded. "Take care. Hopefully, you can get back to England sitting in the correct carriage!"

"You take care of yourself too," I said. "I hope it all works out in Italy."

We said our goodbyes, and I walked out of the terminal building on a warm Parisian evening.

Adjoining the terminal, I found a taxi rank and jumped into the next available cab.

"Where to, Monsieur?" asked the driver.

"I'm not sure. Do you know any cheap but good hotels near the Champs-Élysées?"

"Yes Monsieur. I'll show you a few which I know are exactly what you're looking for."

Nancy looked at the clock on the fireplace consumed with worry. It was 8 o'clock and she decided to call Henry.

"Henry, it's Nancy, how are you?"

"Fine Nancy, hey listen, I spoke to Josh a few hours ago. He said he was all right."

"Did he say where he was?"

"No, but I've got a feeling he won't be back today," replied Henry.

"Yes, he said something about being at the police station. I know he's under arrest, but they can't keep him in like that can they?"

"Yes, they can, depending on the seriousness of the case. It seems his client was highly connected and very important. The police probably want as much information so they can act quickly. I don't think they suspect Josh, but he seems to be the best link they've got at the moment."

"I see, well if you hear from him let me know, I'll try and call him before I go to bed."

Chapter 11
Hotel Deluxe De Paris

The taxi departed the terminal along Boulevard de Magenta and took a right turn into Rue du Saint-Martin; I began to recognise my bearings. After a few minutes, I could see the Chatelet ahead, and it instantly brought back memories of my courtship with Nancy. It was along this stretch of the Seine that I had proposed to her. I had been in Paris on a sales tour and Nancy had joined me for the weekend. Over two days, we wandered the narrow streets of the Left Bank, took a night cruise along the river, partied with the *beau monde* and indulged in the breath-taking architecture. On a warm evening like today, I knew the time was right, and as we walked past the Fountain de Chatelet, right opposite the famous citadel, I got on one knee. When I asked her to marry me, she beamed with an inner radiance. Some of the observant diners alongside the pavement cafés cheered.

No matter how many times one travels to Paris, the stunning boulevards and grand monuments still evoke a celestial charm. For a moment, I had forgotten the reason why I was here; it was the escape that my mind was longing for. Then I felt a sense of guilt. I had lied to Nancy when she had called earlier on the train. But I didn't want her to worry any further.

"We must be nearby?" I said to the taxi driver.

"Yes, there's a place just north of Place de la Concorde, it's called Hotel Deluxe de Paris." *Let us see if it lives up to its name,* I thought.

The taxi drove past Place de la Concorde, and I saw the hotel where I had last stayed. It was Hotel de Bourbon, an eighteenth-century palace that was decorated in a Louis XVI style. Today, I would have to settle for far humbler accommodation.

"Sir, I should let you know, there is a car positioned two cars behind that seems to be following us."

"Are you sure?"

"Yes. I went past Place de Jean-Noel the long way around to double-check. Anyone who knows Paris would not do that. It has been on our tail since the taxi rank."

Damn! I had been too busy admiring the buildings and architecture to even notice. What a silly error of mine. "Forget the Hotel Deluxe—lose that car!" I demanded.

"You know sir, I have been driving around Paris for 20 years. Not only do I know the streets but this is not the first time it has happened."

"Good to know," I muttered with some sense of confidence in this man.

The driver suddenly took a left, and we were along one of the streets parallel to Avenue des Champs-Élysées. The car tailgating immediately mirrored the move.

"*Le cretin,*" cursed the driver. He instantly sped up and overtook two cars. The chasing car could not follow as the oncoming vehicles blocked its path. We were now about four cars further, however, in front of us the lights were changing to red.

"Step on it!"

The driver must have accelerated at least 25 mph, and we managed to clear the lights. But the chasing car was not giving up. We heard a screech and several horns blowing as it clearly went through the red light and narrowly avoided a crash.

The chase continued for at least three to four minutes. I had no idea where I was, but it appeared we had left the centre of town. The erratic driving was making me nauseous but the driver seemed thrilled to be involved in the chase.

There were a greater number of traffic lights on this route and the driver had to turn more often to keep us from coming to a halt. A sense of dread swelled up inside. I had no idea what we'd do if the attackers approached the car.

"Can you see them?" the driver asked.

"No, I can't. But they could be five or six cars behind," I said nervously.

Again a set of lights was about to turn red and the driver sped up. "Oh, the traffic light camera!" shouted the driver.

"I'll pay the fine!"

Our car crossed through the lights as they turned red and the camera flashed. The chasing car must have got stuck behind, as no one else emerged from the traffic junction. Another two minutes of directionless and erratic driving, and it appeared we were safe. The driver calmly pulled into a metered parking space. There was a sense of relief. "We are okay now. Do you still want to go to the Hotel Deluxe?" Without any other alternative popping into my head, I said yes, and we resumed our journey to the hotel.

Whoever was chasing us was not the police. But did they know I was masquerading as Mr Bonham? Probably not—why else did they ask for Mr Rosenburg on the train? It seemed my fake identity had been preserved.

The hotel was on an established touristic route with bed and breakfasts, cheap restaurants and souvenir shops. The driver pulled up outside a large terraced house with a neon sign telling me I had arrived at my destination. He got out and was about to open the boot but stopped mid-way, confused by my sparse belongings. I hadn't even packed an overnight bag! Not having a reservation didn't seem like an issue; it looked like one of those hotels where the vacancy sign is always lit up.

"Thank you," I said, handing the driver 400 Euros. He deemed it an acceptable price for the dramatics that had occurred.

I walked up the steps to the hotel lobby, which was basic but inviting.

"Hello, monsieur."

"I'd like a room for, er, well at least one night," I said.

"That's fine sir, you can always extend your stay, I'll book you in until tomorrow. The rate is 120 Euros per night and breakfast is an additional 10 Euros."

The hotel wasn't deluxe in any way but met the requirement of being clean and reasonably priced. The room was modern but with an old CRT TV. Bright red curtains, a laminated floor and white walls made an attempt at 'contemporary cool'. The bathroom only had space for a small shower, and judging by the lack of bedside menus, no room service.

It was 8:00 p.m., and I decided to freshen up, then get a bite to eat and purchase a change of clothes. So I made my way to the Champs-Élysées, which is one of the grandest avenues of Europe. The evening had turned colder when I reached my destination. Despite the generous pavement on both sides, it was filled with shoppers, tourists and people casually hanging around.

The shops lining the avenue were a mix of upmarket restaurants, 24-hour cafés and chic brasseries, as well as clothing outlets, souvenir shops and even car showrooms. I stopped at a corner café and ordered a croquet monsieur followed by a slice of gateaux; the food was of excellent value. Sitting in the café drinking coffee gave me time to watch passers-by. I looked at swathes of people taking photos, buying goods and talking to one another.

Some people walking past would peer into the café and meet my eyes, but there was one face that looked very familiar. It was of a man whom I had seen recently, however, I couldn't recollect where. I had only caught a fleeting glimpse of him. Maybe it was someone from the train? But then I thought nothing of it. It was time I sent a message to Nancy. 'I won't be home tonight, I'm at the police station but will see you tomorrow, love Josh'. I was hoping she wouldn't doubt me and attempt to check with the station.

Strolling along looking for a men's clothing store, I came across one advertising a huge promotion. I was working on a budget and wished I had also made a credit card in Mr Bonham's name. If my plan to withdraw a small sum from his account went well tomorrow, I'd have enough money to check into the Hotel de Bourbon. I looked around at the surrounding shops before choosing to enter the one with the promotion, but as I went towards its entrance, I thought I saw the same face which I had recognised outside the café.

A second glance at where the face had been, and it had gone. Given the circumstances of my arrival in Paris, I had good reason to be suspicious. Once inside the store, I looked at the discounted rack of suits, shirts and ties. One hundred Euros bought me a jacket and shirt; the suits were so shapeless I had no desire to purchase them no matter how low the price. However, I managed to buy a few items that would help me with my disguise.

I left the shop and conscious that I was possibly being followed again, naturally became more alert. A few glances back, and I couldn't see the face. I continued down the avenue towards Place de la Concorde where I needed to take a left. As I approached my turning I looked back again; no one was following me, but I diverted my course just in case.

I dashed across the road which was overloaded with slow traffic. Once on the other side, I made haste through several large groups of tourists. I had become quite good at being evasive and a sharp turn into a side road and then onto another main road and any doubts of being followed were gone. I jumped into a cab and told the driver to go around a few blocks before returning to the hotel.

Who had been after me earlier today? A plain clothes detective from Scotland Yard? The French police? Mr Bonham? One of Mr Bertrand's bodyguards? I wasn't sure, but one thing was apparent; I was a wanted man. Back at the hotel,

I ensured the window and door were securely fastened and crashed onto the bed. It had been one hectic, surreal day.

My wake-up call was at 8 o'clock, and I got ready to have breakfast at the hotel. The lobby restaurant was relatively empty, the only diners were a young couple and three people travelling on their own. I grabbed the morning paper and sat at the nearest table.

I required a watertight plan for today, but my overriding concern was whether I was able to withdraw a token sum at Credit Union de Paris, posing as Mr Bonham. If successful, I could then arrange for the main loan repayment to be transferred elsewhere, hopefully before it hit the fraudster's account on Monday afternoon.

Halfway through my continental breakfast, I looked absently at the cover page of the newspaper, there was an article about a celebrity footballer having an affair with a hairdresser. I turned the next few pages and with abject horror saw my picture! The headline of an article read: 'Investment banker on the run after client poisoned!'

I hid the paper on my lap and looked at the other diners to see if anyone else was reading it. What should I do now? Given it was a UK publication the chances of someone recognising me here were slim. *Damn,* I thought, *how could it be this big news? People go on the run all the time.*

I had to think quickly now. First, I'd need to do some explaining to Nancy, then there was my poor mother…I was in deep trouble. I picked up the paper again and resumed flicking through the pages, when I got to the end I slapped it face down on the table. The sports headline on the back page read 'Chelsea manager on winning streak', so now I had been promoted to one of those residents in my block that makes it into the paper!

Upon arriving back at my room, my mobile was ringing, it was Nancy. I also had a couple of missed calls from Henry and Hitesh. I answered the phone.

"Hi darling."

"Don't you darling me. Where are you?"

"Look, I'm doing fine. I'm onto something and need to go undercover."

"Why didn't you tell me?"

"It's all very secretive Nancy. I can't give my position away."

"What are you trying to do, Josh? Surely the police can do a better job than you?"

"I know something that they don't, and I can't trust anyone. Darling, please let my mother know I'm well and I'll call you soon."

"The police are sure to come here and question me. What shall I say?"

"Darling this is very important; if they ask if you've spoken to me, don't lie. Say that I called; I don't want you to get in any trouble. It'll all be over in a couple of days. I love you."

Having put down the phone, I realised I couldn't use it again in case it was now being traced. I needed to get a new mobile, but before that, I had to devise a plan for withdrawing Mr Bonham's money. A small withdrawal could be made in cash at the cashier's desk; normally the limit is five thousand Euros without the need for further identification.

The repayment of 24 million would require a transfer to another account or a cheque made up in a third party's name. There was no reason why the money couldn't be transferred to my personal account, although this would probably cement the belief that I was the culprit. Then I had another brainstorm—why not send the money to someone else's account and tell the police I was going to do it? It would at least show that I had no desire to gain from the situation, and demonstrate I was being wrongly accused. Maybe it was a bit far-fetched, but I needed to finalise my plan and stick to it.

It occurred to me I hadn't checked my bogus email account. Now that using Nancy's phone was out of the question, I decided to use one of the communal internet machines that were available in the bar area at the hotel. But I had to be careful; my photo was circulating in public. Given the high-profile nature of the unfortunate victim combined with my failure to show up at the police station, the French Embassy had probably used its clout to advertise me as the villain.

Wearing a cap I had purchased earlier, I walked down to the bar. I desperately wanted a tea, but I thought it was best to head straight for one of the computer screens rather than expose my face needlessly. All the screens were unoccupied, and I chose one in the corner. I logged into the bogus account and to my surprise, there was a reply. It was from Mr Cuthbert-Jones, the real one. The email I had sent had been forwarded to the individual in question. He instantly assumed it was genuine and replied to my bogus email address. His reply read:

Dear Sven,

I received your email but there must be some mistake. I never attended your restaurant on Monday and it's not possible you have my wallet. I double-checked my diary and there is no mention of an inspection at your establishment. However, I can assure you it wasn't me that attended if such an inspection had been booked. Maybe the wallet belongs to someone else? I checked mine and have all my credit cards.

Sorry, I can't be of further help, but it seems you've emailed the wrong person.

Regards,
Mr Cyril Cuthbert-Jones

So, the inspector was an imposter! I was filled with the utmost relief. This was the first piece of evidence—well, legitimate evidence-supporting my claims. What should I do? I forwarded the message to Nancy with a narrative of my theory. If I went missing, this revelation could be followed up by the police. Someone obviously posed as the inspector; I doubt very much the Golden Orchid would have certified the authenticity of the inspection letter. Who would? No one inspects restaurant kitchens for fun. Restaurants expect such letters to land on their doorstep all the time.

Posing as a food inspector, the perpetrator would have had sufficient time and information to add the poison to the correct dish or even several dishes. It was a win-win strategy. Anyone without the allergy would consume their food unaffected. Someone with the allergy would at the very least be hospitalised, possibly killed.

Conscious of someone possibly recognising me, I decided to check out of the hotel. The reception staff had seen me at least three or four times; I needed to find somewhere else to stay tonight. With a satchel over my shoulder, I proceeded to the front desk, paid my bill and walked out.

Shortly after speaking to me, Nancy received a call from the local police station, a policeman was due to visit that morning. So she called her school to inform them that she'd be late and sat waiting in the apartment, consoled by Chela. The doorbell rang and Chela opened the door to an officer of the law.

"Hello, Miss Langham," he said, "I need to go over a few questions with you."

"Certainly."

"When did you last see your fiancé?" he asked.

"Yesterday morning, he was getting ready to go to the police station at noon I believe."

"Did you know he had no intention of getting there?"

"Of course not! Believe me, when I get my hands on him I'm going to make him pay for this!" she said angrily, and then paused. "But my Josh is completely innocent, he's not a murderer or fraudster, do you understand?"

"I'm not accusing your fiancé of murder, but he's now under arrest due to a no-show at the police station, it is a breach of the law. If I may resume, Madam…Do you know of your fiancé's whereabouts?"

"No, although I had a call from him an hour ago saying he's going undercover."

The sergeant laughed out loud. "Undercover," he muttered to himself with a large smile he could not conceal.

"How did he manage to contact you?"

"He had my phone," Nancy admitted.

"Hmm, it's all making sense now, no wonder we could not track his location."

"So, you definitely don't know where he is? Ma'am, may I remind you that I am making a record of this conversation."

"I don't know where he is! I didn't realise he would run off with my phone, oh heck…it has my wedding dress fitting date on it!"

"Must be distressing. But we need to get hold of your fiancé, he may be endangering himself."

"I truly don't know where he is. Maybe you can call him?"

"Thank you for the information. I need to report back to the station. Needless to say, any information you receive please contact me at once," said the policeman, handing over his card and swiftly leaving.

"Chela, I better get to work."

"Yes, you go and don't worry about a thing, Josh knows what he is doing, it'll be okay in the end."

Nancy got ready and on her way down to the foyer, she saw the Chelsea manager with his retinue of bodyguards, smiling at them as they all left the building at the same time. A mass of journalists were gathered outside and the manager stood in front of the expectant crowd.

"Ladies and Gentlemen," he announced with a heavy accent.

"I have a busy day ahead and don't wish to be followed like a zoo animal! I'm going to grab a coffee and will select two journalists for an interview if everyone else promises to leave me alone."

There was a murmur amongst the journalists and then a collective 'Yes, okay'. The manager pointed at a couple of them, and they began walking up Horseferry Road. They stopped outside Drenchin' Doughnuts, eyed up the few empty seats and went inside.

The manager went up to the counter amidst a few stares and whispers from customers at the tables. One of the journalists got in front and offered to get coffee and doughnuts.

"What would you like?" he said turning to the manager.

"Let me see, a cappuccino and the strawberry with honey turmeric please."

"I'll have the same," said the second journalist, slightly unsure what to expect.

The first journalist placed their order and got himself another flavour combination. They sat down at a table for six as the journalists' camera equipment occupied two seats.

"Congratulations on another win, how do you feel?" asked the first journalist.

"It's always good to start with a winning streak, but we both know the club needs to improve its international form," the manager answered while taking a bite of his doughnut.

The first journalist looked at the second to give him his turn to ask a question, but he was too busy munching on his food. So he continued, "Will you change the formation for international games?"

The manager ignored the question and looked at the second journalist. "This doughnut is amazing."

"You're right, that subtle aftertaste of Pernod is phenomenal!"

The first journalist looked confused and slightly embarrassed that his interview wasn't being taken seriously. He picked up his doughnut and bit a chunk off. "Wow, this is tasty stuff," he agreed, "what are those black bits in my dough?"

"Look like poppy seeds to me," said the manager.

The second journalist turned to a staff member who was standing nearby. "Which flavour is this, I can taste Pernod? It's amazing!"

The staff member looked at the doughnut, "I'm not sure, can I take it into the kitchen?" He came out of the kitchen two minutes later. "So sorry gentlemen, that was a trial flavour, it shouldn't have been served to customers, here's a complimentary box of strawberry with honey turmeric."

The first journalist turned to the manager again, "Back to the questions, any formation changes for internationals?"

"Yes, it depends if I want to rest the two key strikers. If so, we'll go for more attacking midfielders."

"What about defence?" asked the second journalist.

"Erm...do you mind if I buy another doughnut, I had a light breakfast."

"Sure," came a joint reply.

The manager went to the counter, this time examining the menu as if it were a post-match analysis of each player.

"How can I help, sir?" came the question from behind the counter.

"Let me see, I'll try the vanilla and cranberry and two lemon and mustard seed, please."

"Sure I'll bring them to the table."

The manager sat back down, expecting to field more football questions.

"What did you order?" asked the second journalist.

"Wait and see, I have very high expectations of this place."

The doughnuts arrived and were devoured in a very short time.

"Mustard seeds in a doughnut, brilliant!" said the second journalist.

"I'm glad I live so close to this place," said the manager, and with that, he got up. "Now gentlemen, I have a business meeting to attend, do excuse me." He left the two journalists at Drenchin', revealing scant information about his team or the proposed formation for the next game.

Chapter 12
Trip to the Bank

Walking along the stretch of the Champs-Élysées where I had been yesterday, I found a mobile phone shop and bought a second-hand phone using my fake ID. The more I pretended to be Mr Bonham, the more realistic my performance would be at the bank. I planned to make the withdrawal during the busy lunch period, when the front desk staff had less time to spend on each customer.

I walked in the direction of the Charles de Gaule Etoile, towards the northern side of the avenue where most of the banks were located, along with designer shops and upmarket apartments. My eyes were scanning faces both in front and behind; paranoia was now my default behaviour. I appeared to be in the clear and soon I was outside Credit Union de Paris.

Having entered the branch, I joined the queue which was moving at a healthy pace. The building's interior was a vast, ornate room with traditional features, which reminded me of my place of work. I was trying hard to look inconspicuous, avoiding eye contact and any conversation with other people in the queue.

Sweat broke out above my brow. I could feel my heart racing faster, and I attempted some deep breathing to put myself at ease. When I got to the front of the queue, my nerves were shaky, but I had to hold it together. What I was doing was highly against my beliefs, not least because I worked in the finance industry and was supposed to uphold the strictest personal integrity.

The buzzer rang and I walked towards cashier number 5. "I'd like to withdraw 3,000 Euros please from my private banking account," I said in a slightly broken voice, passing the female cashier a withdrawal slip.

"Certainly, sir. Can I have some ID?"

I passed her my passport, and she inspected it thoroughly. "Can you tell me the first and third characters of your password?"

"The letter A and the number 1."

"Thank you, sir." She then continued to stare at her screen. "Can you tell me your memorable word or words?"

"Cayman Islands," I recalled instantly. My background reading on the train had served me well.

"Thank you," she said. "Please sign this slip." I did my best to copy Mr Bonham's signature. The cashier added, "By the way, on this account you are normally serviced by the Private Banking team. Next time you can book an appointment with them and needn't queue up. Would you like the team's details?"

"Yes please. In fact, I'm expecting a very large sum of money at noon on Monday—I do need to speak to the team about that."

"Definitely. We only handle smaller transactions here, and anything large needs to be authorised by them anyway." She inspected the signature. "How would you like your cash?"

"In 50 Euro notes please," I said. She handed me the money in an envelope.

"Would you like to speak to the Private Banking team now?" she enquired, simultaneously handing me a paper detailing their contact information.

"No that's fine, I'll call later."

I said goodbye to her and left the branch. Outside, I breathed a big sigh of relief. I had done it. I had to score myself seven out of ten—my nerves almost got the better of me. My next move would be to speak to the Private Banking team in readiness for the large transfer on Monday. I'd call them later in the afternoon.

Being a few thousand Euros richer boosted my mood—at least I could spend the night in a decent hotel! But before choosing a place to stay, I found a stylish clothes store and bought a new suit, shoes and a couple of formal shirts.

The time was 2 o'clock by now and I was feeling hungry. I jumped into a taxi, my destination being Hotel de Bourbon. If I was going to play the part of a rich man, I had to play it properly! The taxi stopped outside the entrance and the doorman opened the car door.

"Any luggage, sir?" he asked.

"No," I replied, handing the taxi driver a 20 Euro note and clutching my shopping. The doorman then held open the grand door of the entrance. "Thank you," I said, entering the stunning gilt and marble reception area. It instantly brought back memories of my last stay. I was in familiar territory and felt a sense of safety. I walked across the polished chequered floor and was greeted by the attentive staff at the front desk.

"I'd like a room for tonight please." I required a couple of nights but thought it was best to book one night at a time.

"Certainly sir, let me take a look." The desk manager paused. "I only have a superior double for 850 Euros per night."

"That's fine. I may need to stay another night."

"Let us know tomorrow by noon," he said. "May I have a credit card imprint please?"

"I'm paying in cash," I said.

"Absolutely," he replied, but I could tell he was a little surprised. "Shall I show you to your room, Monsieur?"

"Not yet, I'm absolutely famished. Do you have a table at La Salle de Bal?"

"I'll check right away…yes, we have. May I take your belongings to the room while you dine?" he said looking at my laptop satchel and shopping bags.

"I'm fine thank you."

He spent another minute completing the room booking and then I followed him to the restaurant.

The dining room of La Salle de Bal was the former ballroom of the palace's previous royal occupants. Its interior was the pinnacle of decorative splendour with frescoed ceilings, crystal chandeliers and different types of marble juxtaposed to create a splendid elegance. This famous dining room had fed Paris' elite for generations, and it held a special memory for Nancy and me; we had dinner there on the night that I proposed.

I must have been the last person to be served lunch, as several tables were already empty and desserts and coffee were flowing to the others. Given my rushed breakfast at Hotel Deluxe, my hunger only increased at the sight of the exquisite food on the menu.

The waiter came over and asked me what I wanted to drink. Tempting though the wine list was, I opted for a bottle of water, I needed my wits about me and could not allow alcohol to dull my reflexes. For an appetiser, I chose seared foie gras with a cherry bouillon and a foie gras terrine, and deboned pigeon and liver with olive oil for the main course.

Whilst eating my food I could not help thinking about the mess I was further creating for myself. Not only had I taken someone else's money, but I was also going on a self-indulgent spending spree. I had to get the message across to the police as to what I was doing and why; they had to understand my motive, and it could only ease any punishment they were going to inflict. I finished lunch, which showcased culinary expertise at its best; I dared not send my compliments to the chef.

I entered my hotel room which seemed like a haven compared with the place I had inhabited yesterday. The windows looked out onto Place de la Concorde and the prospect was simply stunning, with the iconic Eiffel Tower in the distance. The next thing on my plan was to phone Henry. I had to get him to contact the police.

From memory, I dialled Henry's number from my new handset.

"Hello?"

"It's Josh," I said.

"Hey, where the hell are you? Nancy's incredibly anxious."

"I can't say, but I need you to do me a favour."

"I'm not tripping up policemen again! God, he was a heavy fellow—do you know I still have the bruise where he collided with me."

"Thanks mate—but I need you to contact the police."

"Finally your brain is functioning again. Are you going to hand yourself in?"

"Of course not. I'm planning to launder some money, and I need your bank account details."

"What?" he said in disbelief.

"I'm onto something big, a laundering scam—but I'm going to launder the money before the mastermind behind the scam gets his nasty paws on it."

"You're turning deranged," said Henry. "Do you realise you're in deep trouble? Even when you've finished your prison sentence, you'll never get a job in financial services again!"

"Henry, listen to my plan. You need to tell the police that I'm going to deposit a large sum of money into your account. You tell them I'm innocent and plan to steal the money from under the real launderer's nose."

"Why can't you use your account?" Henry asked.

"Because I need to show that I've got nothing to gain from it. Go to the police right now and tell them I've called you."

"Okay. This sounds highly dubious, but I'm involved already now. I really wish I hadn't clashed with that cop, you know they questioned me for an hour afterwards."

"Sorry about that."

"Okay, I'm going along with your plan—but any time you contact me I'll be speaking straight to the police. Do you understand?"

"Yes, fully understood."

"Okay. Hopefully, I've got nothing to lose apart from a drinking pal when you get banged up," he said.

He gave me his account details and promised to call me back once he'd spoken to the law. Glad that I was getting my message across to the police, I could relax a little. I lay on the bed waiting for Henry's call. After a short time, my phone buzzed. Checking the recorded message, Henry had done as instructed, and I fell asleep.

The rush hour had begun and the sound of hooting and beeping from an open window woke me up. It was 4 o'clock, and slightly disorientated, I took a few seconds to remember where I was. I peered outside the window and the late afternoon sun shone from behind the tops of the grandiose buildings. The Eiffel Tower broke the horizon in the distance and pointed to a cloudless sky. Some cars had their dimmer lights on and a policeman was attempting to control the mass of traffic that had slowed to a crawl.

It was time for me to go over the details of Mr Bertrand's account again. I switched on my laptop and looked through his transactions. He had definitely signed an IOU agreement; the signature looked good. What I concluded with Hitesh at Green Park was correct.

Maybe I should call Mr Bertrand—but first I should set up the meeting with the Private Banking team.

I dialled the number provided by the bank cashier, and it was answered within three rings, the hallmark of a good client services team.

"Hello," I enquired, "is that the Private Banking Team?"

"Yes sir, how may I help you today?"

"My name is Mr Bonham. I'd like to meet the team to arrange a transfer as I'm expecting a large loan repayment on Monday."

"Certainly Mr Bonham. We can accommodate you anytime today or before 1:00 p.m. tomorrow as it'll be a Saturday. When would be convenient?"

This is what I liked; proper service where I dictated the time of meetings, not the bank. I'd had enough adventure for one day and decided Saturday would be better.

"I think Saturday morning at 11:00 a.m. would be convenient. I need to set up a transfer of the monies when it arrives in my account."

"No problem, sir."

"Excellent," I said. "11:00 a.m. it is."

"Sir, given that the team hasn't met you in long while, would you like to have a business lunch with the senior account manager afterwards? It would be a good time to discuss your account and any new products you may be interested in?"

"Thank you, but I have another engagement in the afternoon."

"No problem, Mr Bonham; see you at 11:00 a.m. Please also bring your passport, driving licence and transfer paperwork."

"Certainly. Goodbye." I put down the phone. The plan was working.

Before calling Mr Bertrand, I waited momentarily to collect my thoughts and play out in my mind what I wanted to say. I had to say the right things, for I was the last person to see him before he fell ill; who knows what he had been thinking lying on the floor of the Golden Orchid.

If he was conscious now, it was an opportunity to get him on my side. I agonised further for 10 minutes or so before calling him. The phone rang for a long time and then a lady's voice finally answered.

"I would like to speak to Mr Bertrand, please," I said.

"That's a bit difficult right now. Who's calling?"

I paused. "It's Josh Rosenburg."

The lady's voice was filled with melancholy. "Shouldn't you give yourself up?"

"Is this Mme Bertrand?"

"Yes, it is. My husband is still in a coma."

"I'm so sorry, Mme Bertrand. I swear I haven't got anything to do with your husband's poisoning. I swear it!"

"Well, there are a lot of people looking for you. I must go now." She put down the phone and the call terminated, however, I was still listening to a continuous tone, dejected and remorseful. I felt like going back to sleep to try to forget everything. But I had to go on. I needed to stop the real culprit of this heinous crime.

At the hotel lobby, a French police officer approached the hotel reception.

"Excuse me sir, I need your assistance," he said, showing his badge.

The receptionist looked at the French officer. "Yes officer. How can I help?"

"There's a man on the run from England, we believe he may have checked into this hotel. Here's a photo of him—his name is Mr Rosenburg. He was last seen in this vicinity. Do you or the front desk staff recognise him?"

"I'll need to show the picture to the other people that were on duty."

After a few minutes, the receptionist emerged. "Yes, there's a man here who looks like the one in the photo. The desk manager on shift before me saw him enter and book a table at La Salle de Bal. He checked in a few hours ago, went for lunch and then to his room. Obviously, he did not use his real name. He's in Room 202."

"Please stay here and alert hotel security. We have a policeman in the lobby and one covering the back entrance of the hotel. Tell security this man is dangerous, but we don't believe he's armed. I am going up to Room 202 now. There will also be an unmarked policeman covering my back. Do you understand?"

"Yes sir. Should we alert the bar and restaurant staff?"

"Yes, but we have all the corridors secured already."

The French officer dashed to the lift, his unmarked colleague headed towards the stairs.

After my brief conversation with Mme Bertrand, I had a refreshing shower and put on the new set of clothes I'd purchased. Maybe I should pop out and do a bit more shopping? Before I could think any further, there was a loud knock at the door. I froze. Then there was another knock.

"This is the hotel receptionist. Please open the door." I looked through the peephole of the door and I saw a French officer. It seemed the chase was over.

Begrudgingly I opened the door and the officer stood directly in front of me holding a gun, with the receptionist standing some distance behind. "Mr Rosenburg?" he said.

"Yes, that's me."

"You are under arrest on behalf of the UK authorities."

"I know," I said, "but I'm innocent. I'm about to uncover a big scam."

"We can discuss that later," said the officer. "There's a police car waiting outside. I'd like you to accompany me to Place Louis Lepine station. Please do not take any of your belongings."

My memory stick was in my pocket so losing the laptop wasn't a big issue; anyway, I had seen the information I was looking for. I exited the apartment, simultaneously handing the entry card back to the receptionist. I walked coolly through the hotel lounge area with the officer by my side despite receiving piercing stares from onlookers.

The information I had from Hitesh proved there was an attempt to take money from Mr Bertrand, but it wasn't enough to detract the blame away from me. The real Mr Bonham had to reveal himself at some point, and I had to convince the police of that, it was vital to establish who he was. If I had to, I was prepared to run away from the French police to complete my investigation.

At the front of the hotel, the driver of the police car was waiting for us to arrive. I had no chance here. We got into the car. It made its way along the Champs-Élysées, and I was cursing myself for my unsuccessful attempt at remaining elusive.

The officer and the driver said nothing, so I had to break the silence. "Okay, so I have some evidence of a scam, this is what I've been investigating."

"We shall see, Monsieur," came the reply from the officer. "We have been instructed to take you into the station for questioning, but we also need to wait for Scotland Yard to arrive."

The traffic was flowing well and within five minutes we were at the Arc de Triomphe. If anyone has driven around this monument, they know that it's one of the most difficult roundabouts to negotiate in the world. It has 12 exits and probably 10 lanes! The police car entered the roundabout, and we were in the middle of all the lanes. There were cars stacked on either side, moving at variable speeds. Some were driven by confident drivers, a few hire vehicles shifted with no sense of direction and others drove hesitantly. Many cars bore wounds of unfortunate clashes—not surprising as they had the lane discipline of a balloon that had been fully filled and then released.

The police car then tried to head for exit 8 or 9 and began veering right, but before we got to the outer lane there was a deafening thud and the sound of crushing metal could be heard. The impact shook the police car, and it slid 90 degrees as the driver braked. Luckily, I was not on the side of the crash, but the officer who had arrested me seemed slightly concussed. The driver was sitting in shock as other cars made their way around the two vehicles that had collided.

This was my moment to escape! Not wasting a second, I opened the door and fled. The crash had slowed down the traffic, and I was able to dodge cars across the roundabout and run into one of the exit roads.

The road I ran down was called Avenue de Wagram. I turned into a side road on my left and straight into a café. *I'd be safe here for at least a few hours,* I thought. Sipping a cup of coffee, my mobile rang and I recognised the number as Henry.

"Hi," I said.

"Hi Josh, guess what?"

"What?"

"The new manager of Chelsea loves Drenchin' Doughnuts!" he exclaimed.

"And you had the nerve to call me deranged! What are you on about you fool?"

"Well, it's a bizarre headline but the Chelsea manager apparently had an interview at Drenchin' and couldn't help but praise their products! Everyone's talking about the place and the stock has gone through the roof!"

"Glad to hear it," I said miserably. "What did the police say when you spoke to them?"

"Oh yeah, they thought you were trying to stall their investigation and told me to tell you that money laundering is a serious crime!"

"Look, I don't want them to trace this call so bye!" I said hastily switching off my phone.

Back on the run, I still had to survive a couple of days. Maybe changing my appearance would be a good idea, again! With this in mind, I jumped into a cab and directed the driver to the Les Halles district, intentionally avoiding the Champs-Élysées.

At the shopping precinct, most of the fashion stores were for women, but I found a men's retailer and purchased a completely new outfit. I still had to look smart for the bank meeting and opted for a blazer and shirt, as well as changing my shoes for a comfortable pair with a rubber sole.

Having sorted out my clothes, I stumbled across a hair salon and had my hair highlighted and cut back. By this time it was 8 o'clock, and I was mindful of finding another place to stay. Somewhere fancy wasn't an option, it was best to stick to a small, discreet hotel.

Outside the precinct, a taxi driver suggested a suitable place, and I was taken to a low-budget guesthouse. The man at the front desk led me to a room on the third floor overlooking the street. Inside, the room was small, with a stained blue carpet. The double bed left little room to manoeuvre around. The ensuite bathroom could have done with re-grouting and a clean, but the real annoyance was the sound of a metro train passing by every three or four minutes. I settled down on the bed and contemplated my fate.

Not being fussy about dinner, I left the guesthouse. At the top of the road, I had seen a few cafés and I chose one which looked busy. I went up to the bar and ordered a drink, unsure what to eat. I hadn't been sitting long when I heard my name being called.

"Josh, hey! How you doin'?"

I turned around in shock. It was James Evergreen, someone with whom I'd worked shortly after he'd graduated. James was initially assigned as a junior analyst at Omega, and I had been his graduate mentor. He also did a stint on my desk with the client services team. Meeting him in this bar under the current circumstances was not my idea of a reunion.

"What are you doing here?" I asked before he could ask me.

"I'm working for a French brokerage firm. I moved over here with my parents about five years ago—well, they actually live in St Tropez now, and I moved to Paris."

"Nice, how are you finding it here?"

"It's great! I head up an Emerging Markets team. Moved from being an analyst to a trader. Thanks for all that mentoring back in the day! It must have registered somewhere in my empty head!"

"Well done. I thought there was trading material in you."

"Hey, do you fancy a quick beer?"

I considered my options. I knew I could trust him. He was one of those guys that had shone out of a promising group of graduate intakes when he joined. Being his mentor, I had trained him on the basics of the company business model, how Omega made money, how to deal with clients, the rules and regulations of the workplace, the investment management process and so on. He had been keen to learn, and I knew my time spent with him would not be wasted. I had helped him plan his career path and determine his occupational aspirations. I knew he was grateful for all that I had done for him. There was no way he would go against what I said.

"A beer would be good. Where is your brokerage based?"

"Oh, in the La Défense district, where a lot of finance companies are located. I pop down here for a drink sometimes—my apartment is only up the road. How about you—are you based in France now?"

I paused and decided I might as well come clean straight away. He had to remain quiet about my whereabouts, and I needed him to trust me. Any sightings of me to the police, and I could easily be residing in a French jail. Given his connections in the same financial circles as me, he either knew I was on the run and wasn't saying anything out of politeness or would have found out shortly anyway.

"I'm investigating a fraud at Omega," I announced. "Well, in fact, I'm trying to clear my name."

"What? How did that come about?" he asked, visibly taken aback by what I had said. Obviously, he was not aware of the headlines I had generated.

"It's a long story, but at the moment I am a wanted man in France and am working undercover. Please can I have your word that you won't say anything?"

"Of course, so what's exactly happened?"

"Well, it's a difficult one. One of my clients was poisoned and the finger points to me."

"What," James said, "the actual hell!"

"I went out for lunch with an important client, and he passed out during our meal. Then I noticed some dodgy transactions between him and another client, they had an IOU agreement. But listen to this, days before the payment is due, the client owing the money allegedly gets poisoned. The police have made up numerous reasons why I had cause to do it and now I'm having to prove my innocence. From what I have found, the counterparty to the IOU seems highly mysterious."

"Definitely an inside job. You know, bet someone's manipulated records from within the firm?"

"That's a good point James. Yes, that's what I concluded."

"Absolutely barmy!" he muttered, still with a look of disbelief.

"Let's talk about something else," I said. "Why did you leave Omega?"

"I couldn't stand the politics. Some of the traders took the glory for my analysis, and it wasn't fair. Every time I recommended some really good stocks to the investment managers, the traders would take the credit. Needless to say, it always happened around bonus time!"

“It can be tough. Some of the traders only see things for themselves, there’s no collaboration.”

“A few of them were plain horrible,” he continued. “Yeah, Miles being the worst of the lot. Well, when my year-end bonus wasn’t what it should have been, I quit after three years. That’s when I got a junior role at my current employer.”

Meeting James was a welcome relief, given the few days I’d had. Having a cold beer in a bar with a friend brought some kind of normality back to my life.

“How’s work now?” I asked.

“Things are going reasonably well. Obviously, we’ve not had a good year due to the financial conditions but at least I have a job and work with people I like.”

“That counts for a lot, my friend,” I reassured.

Our conversation went on for quite a while and James recommended eating at the café attached to the bar. We caught up on old times over a chicken and sausage *cassoulet*, which proved to be a hearty meal. After ordering coffee around midnight and exchanging email addresses, we went our separate ways. I got back to the guesthouse and immediately settled for bed.

Chapter 13
Help, He's Trying to Kill Me!

I must have been tired as the reverberations from the metro train below had failed to wake me up; instead, it was the cleaner banging on the door at 9 o'clock. As I got up, I kept wondering how the police had located me so quickly at Hotel de Bourbon. Was it from a sighting, or by tracing my brief call to Mrs Bertrand? Either way, I decided not to take chances with my mobile. Today, I had to visit the Private Banking team at Credit Union de Paris and arrange the big transfer for Monday. Wearing my new clothes, I left the guesthouse around 10:00 a.m. and returned to the Les Halles area, about a twenty minute walk from the bank.

A jam-filled croissant sufficed as breakfast, after which I made my way to the bank's headquarters on the Champs-Élysées. I hadn't noticed what an imposing building it was, made from fine stone and in keeping with the Hausmann inspired apartment blocks nearby. On my first attempt at entering the building, I lost my nerve and walked straight past. It gave me some time to peer through the entrance door although this did nothing to dampen my anxiety. I had to go through with this and with a bout of conviction too. On my second attempt, I entered, still feeling tense.

"Good morning. I have an appointment today with the Private Banking team at eleven."

"Let me see—yes, morning Mr Bonham and welcome. Sandrine will be down in a moment. Please take a seat."

As I sat waiting, it occurred to me I was now playing the part my clients would normally play. How strange! The lift opened and a smart lady wearing a blue blouse approached me, making eye contact.

She extended her hand. "Bonjour. My name is Sandrine."

"Nice to meet you."

"And you too, Mr Bonham. Please follow me—we're on the second floor." I duly followed, not sure whether to engage in small talk in case I said something I shouldn't. "How long are you in Paris?"

"Oh, only for a few days. It's purely for business."

"I see." She led me into a modern-looking meeting room.

I sat down at a polished glass desk. The seats were black leather and very comfortable. The walls were covered with abstract artworks and a tall window looked onto the shopping avenue below. The obligatory teas, coffees and pastries were nicely presented on a sideboard.

"Before we begin—tea or coffee?" A waiter entered the room.

"A coffee please, no sugar."

The waiter attended to my request and also poured Sandrine a hot drink. After placing a few biscuits on the table, he left the room.

"I understand you want to make a bank transfer request?" asked Sandrine, opening a laptop.

"Yes please. I have a large loan repayment arriving on Monday and need to give a new instruction."

"Okay, we can certainly look into that. First of all, can I go over some security questions?"

"Sure," I replied, far more confident than I had been yesterday.

She took my account details, and then I showed her my ID, which she spent a considerable amount of time inspecting. To hide my unease, I picked up a biscuit and took a bite, followed by a few sips of my coffee.

"Can you tell me of any recent transactions on your account?"

"Yes, I withdrew 3,000 Euros yesterday when I arrived in town. Other than that I have not used the account."

"You said you are expecting a large sum of money? May I see the documentation for that, please?" I produced a copy of the loan agreement. "One moment sir—I need to check it with someone else." She left the room for what must have been ten minutes. I could do nothing but just sit there, look out of the window and finish my coffee.

Then she returned, smiling. "Great, that's what we have on file; all is good. Tell me, how are the Cayman Islands this time of year?"

"As you can imagine, nice, but hurricane season is coming up!"

"Oh, dear! And finally, please may I have characters two, three and seven from your account password."

I answered all the security questions with ease. She began typing on her laptop. "So, it appears you already have a transfer which was set up at the Credit Union de Paris branch in the UK, at least a year ago."

I had expected this question. Needless to say, it had been set up by the real Mr Bonham.

"Yes, I need to change it now. Can you remind me where I instructed? Was it the account in Switzerland?"

"No, it is being paid to a company registered in the British Virgin Islands."

"Oh, yes," I said. "I need to change it. The money will now be invested in a new green energy company. It's based in the UK—I know the CEO, a Mr Henry Jones."

"Please may I have the new payment details?"

I handed over a slip of paper with Henry's property business account details.

"Thank you," said Sandrine. "So to confirm you want to change the transfer details we have on record for Monday's transaction?"

"Yes please." After entering the instructions into her laptop, Sandrine asked if there was anything else that she could do to assist.

"No," I said.

"Good, rest assured as soon as the bank receives the 24 million Euros, approximately around noon, we will transfer it to the new account you have specified," Sandrine confirmed.

"You've been a great help, thank you. I better be on my way now."

Once the meeting had finished, I recognised that the next objective was to remain inconspicuous for another day or so. If I could manage that, I could outwit the real Mr Bonham. Given my track record, keeping out of sight was proving to be difficult, even staying at different hotels hadn't worked. The best strategy might be to keep on the move and stay in crowded places. I could easily spend a day in Montmartre with its famous basilica. Not yet decided, I wandered aimlessly through the side streets. I came across a metro station and made up my mind to go to Montmartre.

I walked up the steep road that approaches the Sacre Coeur cathedral from Anvers station. The sight of the magnificent structure ahead was breath-taking. Standing at the very base of the hill on which the cathedral is perched, I had a choice of taking a cable car or the steps. The latter provided an opportunity to pass time, to leisurely spend the remaining hours of the day before getting closer to the end of the painful journey I had taken.

Upon reaching the top, I stopped to look back and appreciate the superb views of the city. I planned to first go inside the cathedral before taking a walk past the market stalls and artisan boutiques in the surrounding streets.

Inside the cathedral, it was a real sanctuary. I could hear the low hum of prayers near the pulpit, and I gasped at the sheer intricacy of the decorative artwork that adorned the walls. Tourists were going around the perimeter in a clockwise fashion, but I sat down on a pew. Closing my eyes, I thought about Mr Bertrand and his wife, they were the real victims in all this, and as I sat there, offered my prayers for their wellbeing.

I then joined the other tourists and walked around the interior. When I stepped outside, the sun was hidden by threatening clouds and the view over the city was cast in shadow.

Sandrine returned to her desk, ready to finish earlier as it was a Saturday. Her phone rang.

"Hello, this is Charles Bonham, and I'd like to speak to someone regarding some cash movements on my account."

"Hello Mr Bonham, it's Sandrine. Do you want to make some changes from our meeting just now?"

The caller paused, confused and out of breath. "Meeting? I didn't attend any meeting with you! I am the real Mr Bonham! There is a guy posing as me. A fraudster who is on the run from England. He is in the papers, a wanted man! I did not meet you today."

Sandrine was taken aback, "Who is this? Is this some kind of joke? I met Mr Bonham an hour ago, a very nice man."

"He is an imposter," shouted the caller. "Do not do anything on the account, I beg you, your bank is making a big mistake. He is going to take my money!"

Sandrine hesitated. "Sir, if you say you are the real Mr Bonham, then you need to prove it on Monday morning. I can't do so today as the Compliance team and Systems Security are off at the weekends."

"I'm telling you, I am the real Mr Bonham!" pleaded the caller.

"Sir, may you come into the Champs-Élysées branch at 9:00 a.m. on Monday. It is very important that you do so. I am going to freeze the account and report it to the bank's security team straight away. I will meet you along with our Head of Compliance and Systems Security. Until then all transactions will be frozen."

"I see," replied the caller, a lot calmer now but still agitated. "Okay, I'll see you at 9:00 a.m. Please take a look at Friday's edition of The Daily Metro paper in the UK, you will see the imposter's face. Surely you'll recognise him?"

"Certainly, I will. See you on Monday, Mr Bonham," said Sandrine, terminating the call. Could this have been a genuine call? Was this a serious error on her part? She had carried out all the necessary checks; no one had ever fooled her like this. Thinking quickly she brought up Mr Bonham's details on her computer system. Mr Bonham's mobile number had changed about five years ago, the same time as the address change. She dialled the number.

"Hello?" came a reply. She recognised the voice instantly, it was the caller who had dialled a moment ago.

"Hello again, this is Sandrine. I'm just doing some checks."

"Yes, I told you, I am the real person. You have the correct mobile number."

"I got it," she said. "I'll see you on Monday."

Sandrine immediately put a block on any outgoing transactions from Mr Bonham's account.

Walking through the pedestrianised lanes next to the cathedral I saw some fascinating shops; there was one that made hand-painted dinner sets. Another was a temple to luxury briefcases, wallets and pens. Nancy would have loved the shop with an extravagant display of silk scarves and pashminas. It was tempting to make a purchase, and I promised myself that if I got out of this mess, I'd bring Nancy here for a shopping trip.

Peering through the window display of a wine merchant, a reflection in the glass caught my eye. It was a face. A face that I'd seen on my first day on the Champs-Élysées. I don't know how he had found me, but he was here! The pressure I had felt earlier in the morning returned as my pace quickened, and I began walking towards the metro station.

The man started following me, albeit some distance behind. There was no need to appear discreet. This man was intent on getting me and I started to run, accelerating as fast as I could downhill.

Maybe I could lose him by going back to higher ground near the Cathedral, I thought. Having faith in my jogging prowess, I kept running at speed and then commenced my ascent along a narrow street. I was drawing a lot of attention as shopkeepers and pedestrians stopped to take a look.

Running up towards the Cathedral I knew where I was going. Behind it was a set of very steep steps descending to ground level again. I took fairly large strides, almost lunges as I increased the distance between myself and the man chasing. I was beginning to tire but my pace remained steady.

"Hey, watch it," shouted a woman behind me as I brushed past a group of musicians readying themselves for an outdoor performance. I quickly glanced back and noticed the man was out of sight. Had I outrun him? Another sharp left and I entered a road full of souvenir shops. At this stage, I was panting quite loudly but decided that hiding in a shop to catch my breath wasn't a good idea.

So I continued running, but slower. I made it to the top of the hill again with the Cathedral to my right. Large crowds at the top forced me to adopt a walk. Constantly looking backwards, I had lost the man. But I still had to hide; for all I knew he may have an accomplice.

I was now at the rear entrance of the Cathedral and made my way down the steep steps behind it. Once at the bottom, I took a left onto the main road that led towards the legendary Moulin Rouge club. I hadn't walked for longer than a minute when a hundred metres ahead of me I saw the man again. Reluctantly I made a U-turn back in the direction of the steep steps.

The man gave chase for a second time. I turned a corner and travelling too fast, tumbled over several times. The man was making up ground quickly as I got to my feet. I briefly stared at him, now only fifty meters away. He slowed down and reached inside a pocket and pulled out a gun.

I froze in panic, but at the same time a large group of students spilt out onto the road, and he was forced to hide it. I sprinted again, this time running away from the Cathedral. I couldn't keep this up and needed a rest. Ahead of me, I saw a building with a group of students loitering outside.

It was a college, an Ecole d'Anglais to be precise. If the man had a gun, my best bet was to stay in a crowd. So I slowed down and entered the college, hoping that it was unlikely for a firearm to be used with so many witnesses around.

Luckily the foyer was quite busy, and luckier still was the fact that there was no barrier to enter the main part of the school.

The receptionist at the entrance looked at me as I desperately avoided her gaze. "Hey Mister, can I help you?" she shouted over the numerous conversations that were taking place. Ignoring the question I ran down the main corridor and then turned into an adjacent hallway. Several doors were leading off the hallway, widely spaced apart. I could see they were labelled: Lecture Room 4, Lecture Room 5 and so on.

I barged into Lecture Room 6 and fifty or so students including the lecturer turned their heads. Looking sheepish, I walked towards the end of the aisles and sat down. Not to draw further attention I decided to remain there as well as catch my breath. After a harsh stare, the lecturer continued. "Last week I was talking about commodity pricing using a bootstrap model. In today's lecture, I will extend the pricing theory. Let me show you the equation for the pricing model." He began writing on the whiteboard what appeared to be a very complicated equation.

God, I thought, *this is worse than the Investment Management meetings I normally attend.* The lecturer continued for another couple of minutes and then the door burst open. It was the man who had been chasing me. He looked around and saw me at the back of the theatre. Without any delay, he sat down at the first available seat.

What was I going to do now? Behind me, I could see a fire exit. That was my only viable means of escape. Climbing over students to get to the other side of the aisle wasn't an option. The man kept looking at me. I gave him a cold stare, then I remembered where I had seen him. Although he was clean-shaven without any glasses, it was the food inspector! Yes, the inspector from the Golden Orchid. The height of the man, his body shape and his face were consistent with the person I remembered at the restaurant while patiently waiting for my turn to be seated. He turned around again.

"That man has a gun!" I shouted at the top of my voice, pointing at him. "In his jacket, he has a gun!"

"He is wanted for murder!" replied the man pointing back at me.

The students stared at us, some giggled and others were appalled.

"Can you both leave my lecture theatre please!" shouted the lecturer.

"I'm telling you this man has a gun!" I shouted again.

"I'm going to call the police! Now, will the pair of you let me continue with my lesson?"

I stood up, the man remained seated looking at me with a scowl. Suddenly, I made a dash for the fire exit, and he immediately followed suit. Some students got up to see what was going on. I crashed through the fire doors, causing the alarm to sound.

The ensuing chaos was to my benefit as groups of students began emptying lecture theatres. The man giving chase struggled to push past the dense crowds forming in the corridors. I had the advantage of being the first to leave the lecture room and was now close to the building's entrance. I sped past the reception desk and emerging back on the road, I ran towards the Cathedral again.

I got to the foot of the steep steps and began my ascent, leaping two or three steps at a time. Glancing behind me, I saw the man at the bottom. He stopped and pulled out his gun, took aim and fired a shot. It missed, and I resumed the ascent. *Damn,* I thought, *I really am out of my depth.*

Exhausted from the previous chase, my pace was sluggish but still reasonably swift. At the top, I arrived at a cobbled road. The man with the gun was gasping for air midway up the steps, and I managed to pull further away. Turning left into a two-way road I made the mistake of looking backwards while attempting to scale a high kerb at the same time.

Twisting my foot, I hit the ground with my arms outstretched. My palms scrapped against the pavement, and I narrowly missed smashing my head on the hard ground. This gave the gunman enough time to get within shooting distance, and he slowed down, raising the gun to my head. As I picked myself up, it was too late, the man was towering over me, arm outstretched with the barrel of the gun touching the tip of my hair.

"Get up Mr Rosenburg—or should I say Mr Bonham?"

I looked at him, at this proximity I was certain it was the food inspector. Without warning, a black Fiat screeched to a halt right next to us, filling the air with tyre smoke. We both turned around at this unexpected interruption.

"Freeze!" shouted a man from inside the car holding a pistol. The food inspector ignored him and got ready to pull the trigger, but he was too slow. The man in the car fired a shot and the bullet went through the food inspector's neck.

He slumped to the ground. I looked at the man who had fired the gun with absolute terror. Things had got very serious—maybe there was more than one person after the money? Before the man in the car could react, I ran faster than I had done before. I'm not sure in which direction I went but ended up on Rue des Trois Freres. Here, I saw a cab and leapt in. I had escaped.

The man driving the black Fiat walked up to the food inspector, who was clearly dead. He emptied the food inspector's pockets and replaced them with a passport, wallet and driving licence in the name of Mr Josh Rosenburg. Leaving the gun still firmly clasped in the food inspector's hand, he calmly got back into his car and drove away.

A few moments later a nearby shopkeeper and a few customers ran up to the body, promptly calling the police.

Chapter 14
At a Dead End

The cab moved slowly through the early evening traffic. I was constantly looking out of the window for the black Fiat, I felt I had unearthed a can of worms and was compounding an already grave situation. *Surviving the remaining 24 hours was going to be tough; I'd be safer in a police station,* I thought. It appeared that no matter where I hid, I would be found. The relentless chase was getting to me. I didn't have the energy to carry on like this.

"Where are we going, Monsieur?" asked the cab driver.

"Take me to Boulevard de Hausmann," I replied. I decided again that hanging out in a busy place would be the safest thing for me. Switching on my phone I could see Nancy had tried calling a few times. Henry must have given her my new number.

The cab driver tried to make conversation, but his English was poor, and I was too distracted to partake in polite chat. It was turning dark, and the roads were full of people going about their weekend business. I could visualise the headlines back home: "Fraudster on the run kills an accomplice," or something that implicated me with the food inspector. I had to decide where to stay the night. It wasn't worth returning to the hotel by the Metro station, plus, I needed a good night's sleep without the constant racket from passing trains.

When the cab arrived at my destination, before reaching for my money, I checked that I still had the memory stick in my jacket pocket, which it was. I paid the driver and went straight into Galleries Lafayette. I found myself wandering again. The only difference between now and this afternoon was that it was separated by a murder.

Inside the store, I gravitated to the bar on the first floor. It was a Champagne bar, but I was in no mood to celebrate having escaped death! I ordered a glass of red wine. My overriding thought was to call Nancy. But first I needed to make sense of the events that had just taken place.

Why did the food inspector want to kill me? Why did someone kill the food inspector? Were they aiming for me but happened to be a bad shot? I ordered another drink and sat at the bar in a daze trying to disentangle everything. Realising that I hadn't eaten lunch, I decided to leave. It was 7:00 p.m. and walking along the main boulevard, I stumbled across one of my favourite burger chains. I couldn't resist and went inside. My head was pulsating at this point and the hunger didn't help. I found a small table and quickly ordered a double cheeseburger. Whilst eating, my thoughts circulated endlessly. I left the restaurant, continuing my walk along Boulevard de Hausmann.

Still conflicted about where to spend the night, I entered a noisy bistro. Sitting on a stool at the end of the counter, I sipped a coffee and watched TV, although the volume was too low to be audible. Unexpectedly, a news bulletin came up; it was about the shooting!

I got up with a numbing shock, but then I should have known, it had happened in one of the most prominent tourist spots in broad daylight. As I couldn't hear the TV, I managed to read the scrolling headlines which were in English. "Fraudster on the run from the UK has been shot!" the headline read. It went on to say a Mr Rosenburg had entered France illegally on Wednesday and was critically wounded in a shootout.

What! I exclaimed in my head. Now events had gone too far. They were appealing for witnesses and a blurry image of the driver of the black Fiat was shown on the screen. Appeals for the person who had run away from the scene—in other words, me, were also being made! I finished my drink and had made up my mind; it was time to give myself up, but in the morning. My biggest issue now was to find a safe place to sleep and figure out what convoluted explanation I'd give to the police. I was at a dead end.

I walked towards the Arc de Triomphe, heading for a stretch of hotels off the main roundabout where I had stayed as a student. I knew I could get a room in one of them. En route, I picked up a hat from one of the souvenir shops in a poor attempt at being disguised.

The hotel I chose was at the corner of a five road junction. It gave me a few options in which to escape in case I had to make a swift exit. Entering the hotel, I requested a room. As I had guessed, there was more than one vacancy, and I was presented with a choice of two rooms.

I selected the one on the ground floor, covering all possibilities in case I had to jump out of a window. My mind had switched to an irrational line of thinking; I was behaving completely out of character.

The hotel room was brightly lit, with windows on adjoining walls given its position at the corner of the building. Its interior was smarter than I had envisaged, with high ceilings and impressive plasterwork. All I wanted to do was wait until tomorrow and report myself to the police. There was only one day left to tell them about the fraud that might occur on Monday, and they had to believe me.

After a sound night's sleep, I woke up refreshed on Sunday morning. The endless chases and running the day before had given me aching muscles, but my mind was relieved of the anxiety I had felt previously. As I got up, preparing to hand myself in, the gravity of the situation dawned upon me. If I couldn't prove myself innocent, or couldn't convince the police to investigate elsewhere, there was a real chance I could end up in prison.

This unedifying thought made me think of another irrational thing to do. Today might hail the last day of my freedom for a long time. If I was going to be locked up, I should have a fond memory of my last meal as a free man. *It had to be a grand breakfast,* I thought, *at La Salle de Bal!* Then I would go to the police station. It was decided, and I checked out and hailed a taxi.

"Where to Monsieur?" asked the driver.

"Hotel du Bourbon, please."

The taxi took a leisurely cruise along the Champs-Élysées. I expected less traffic and pedestrian foot flow at this time on a Sunday, but I was wrong. However, it was welcome as I calmly contemplated the surroundings and partook in people watching. The taxi stopped outside the hotel and a porter opened the door.

"Thank you," I said, walking towards reception.

"May I have a table for one for breakfast, please?" The female receptionist replied that a table was available and asked for my name.

"I'm Josh; Josh Rosenburg." She then gestured towards the restaurant.

The head waiter warmly greeted me and showed me to my table. As I sat down, I noticed the receptionist peering through the entrance of the restaurant. Maybe she recognised me from my last visit?

The breakfast menu catered for those who only wanted to peck at a fruit salad to a full-on royal feast. I opted for something in between, the American

Breakfast. Waiting for my food to arrive gave me time to fully appreciate the ambience of such a fine place.

This type of luxury might only be a dream in a few hours. In the distance, I saw the receptionist reappear and walk over to a waiter. I did not care what was going on; I was handing myself in. Breakfast arrived with all the paraphernalia befitting such an indulgent experience. Service was exemplary and the staff courteously asked after me every ten minutes or so.

At the entrance of the restaurant, two men now appeared, one was a uniformed French officer and the other plain-clothed. They briefly spoke to my waiter, who then approached me, handing me a note of paper. It read: "Please make your way to us; there is a police car outside, we are taking you to the police station."

Wonderful, I thought, *even arrests in this restaurant are elegant and refined!* Upon finishing breakfast, I left a hefty tip on the table and began approaching the two men. The waiter, noticing I had paid the bill, turned to me. "Hope you had a nice breakfast, Mr Rosenburg."

"Indeed, please send my compliments to the chef!" I requested, and then recalled how good lunch had been on Friday. "And also for lunch on Friday, the pigeon was excellent!" The waiter nodded as the two men stared at me with some amusement. As I got closer to them, the plain-clothed gentleman introduced himself.

"Bonjour, I am Inspector Renee from the special branch, French police. We need you to come with us right now. There is a police car waiting outside."

"Certainly," I replied. "I assume I am under arrest?"

"Let's discuss things at the police station." I walked past the receptionist and gave her a big smile, which was not reciprocated. Then I was led to the police car.

Once inside, I was handcuffed. "No jumping out this time eh?" joked the uniformed officer.

The car set off, taking the exact route it had two days earlier. After negotiating the Arc de Triomphe successfully, it wasn't long before we arrived at the station. I entered, handcuffed and surrounded by the two policemen.

"One moment sir," replied the officer at the desk. He took me to a room and told me to sit down, duly freeing my hands and closing the door.

The door then swung open and Inspector Renee appeared. He took a deep look at me. "Can I see your ID? Who are you?" I immediately gave my true details and also presented my real and fake IDs. The inspector gave me a glaring stare, then sat back in his chair and laughed. "You are no longer under arrest!"

"What! You mean I'm a free man?" It was still hard to take in what he had just said. I was preparing myself for mind-numbing days behind bars and meagre nourishment. But there were so many unanswered questions. Hopefully, after today, I'd have all the answers.

"Not quite; we need your help. So we are going to hang onto your real passport in case you decide to do something else."

"What do I need to do?" I asked.

Another two officers entered the room, closing the door behind them.

"Morning. I'm Officer Du Pre. I will go over the plan," said one of the officers. The other officer introduced himself as Officer Paul.

The inspector then resumed the conversation. "We believe the man who tried to shoot you was an accomplice of the real mastermind. We did not want to kill him but had to when you placed your own life in danger by being so stupid." I did not reply.

"We validated what your friend Henry told us about your meeting at Credit Union de Paris. It is clear you set up a transfer to Henry's account, and together with other evidence this eliminated you as a suspect. You have nothing to gain and neither does your best friend. Also, we think you are right with your hunch, there is room to believe that a loan agreement between a Mr Bonham and Mr Bertrand is fraudulent. But we don't know for sure. We can't make any arrests until we have concrete evidence."

"I see," I replied.

"But we are closer to identifying the real Mr Bonham. French police managed to retrieve a recent photo—I say recent, but it's from about six years ago from his brother, whom we tracked down at a Champagne producer in Reims. His brother mentioned that he had last seen Charles Bonham before his trip to the UK six years ago. We have nothing about his time in the UK," explained Inspector Renee.

"So, is he a missing person?"

"No. No one has reported him missing, and we see a trip to the Cayman Islands on his records in the past five years."

"Also, we got hold of Steve Chatsworth, an ex-colleague of yours. It seems he met Mr Bonham many years ago. But Steve is working in the States nowadays, so we called him. He said he couldn't recall accurately what his ex-client looked like; he only met him twice, and he literally has met hundreds of clients since then. We need to know more about the loan agreement between the two businessmen at Omega. That's where we need your help to piece everything together."

"Well, what I know is pretty much what I told Henry and my fiancée. I think there is a conspiracy to commit fraud, but Mr Bertrand cannot confirm that. Do you know how he is by the way?"

"I believe he is still in a coma," interrupted Officer Du Pre.

"What a shame! All I know is that if the money is transferred out of Mr Bonham's account on Monday, it is lost forever. It could end up anywhere, the Cayman Islands, Switzerland, who knows where?"

"But if the loan agreement is genuine, then we have no right to intercept it," said Inspector Renee.

"This is true," I said. "The rules are fair; until we prove there is the intent of wrongdoing, it should be business as usual. I wouldn't want my clients' affairs to be interrupted if there was no valid reason to do so."

"Unfortunately, the person who might detect this crime is in a hospital bed in London. If your friend Mr Bertrand dies, we may never know the truth. I believe the fraudster intended to kill Mr Bertrand; it would be the best way of getting the money without raising any difficult questions. As it happens, Mr Bertrand is in no position to help."

"So do you believe the food inspector—I mean, the person that was shot yesterday—poisoned my client?" I asked.

"Yes, that's what we believe. In the Golden Orchid kitchen, there are no cameras pointing at the kitchen staff, instead, they look towards the back door and the entrance to the dining room. Luckily, the video footage clearly showed the food inspector entering the kitchen. Together with the email you sent to your fiancée the other day, we know that the kitchen inspection was fake. We are still tracing the food inspector's identity, and hopefully, we can find the source of the poison."

"I knew it! That's exactly what I concluded," I exclaimed. "Can I speak to my fiancée, please?"

"Yes, but after we have discussed the schedule for tomorrow."

"Tomorrow? What am I expected to do?"

"We need you to assist us. Don't worry, you won't end up being shot at! Given your handy work rearranging Mr Bonham's payment instructions, he will now need to visit Credit Union de Paris on Monday morning in person. If he doesn't show up, we can put an alert on his account if any large withdrawals are attempted. If he does show up, it's either the real person or the fraudster. We…"

"Surely a visual check against his most recent photo would give you that?" I interjected. "Unless a client is well known and recognised by their client representative, a photo check against a driving licence or passport is mandatory. Visual identification is key." I had a hunch that if Mr Bonham had not been seen for five years, the chances were that the person who last met him at Credit Union de Paris would not be the one meeting him on Monday.

"Yes," said the inspector. "But this is why we went to great lengths to track down his brother so that we could instantly compare the real person with the photo."

"That sounds good; if the ID and photos match, then we have to conclude it is the real person. Strangely, he has been off the radar for such a long time."

"Yes, this is another avenue of our investigation. We are unsure of his whereabouts, for all we know he may be dead!"

"Interesting trail of thought," I said.

"The good thing is he must show up now. After your meeting yesterday, the bank is on high alert. But they are quite uncomfortable with our plan; we could damage their reputation, so we need to tread carefully."

"So what exactly is the plan?" I enquired. "Where do I fit in?"

"Maybe we take a break now and you can call your fiancée?" suggested the inspector.

"Yes, good idea."

"Okay, we'll see you back in one hour; you are free to use the lounge area opposite, but you cannot leave the station. Is that clear?"

"Yes, but what about tonight?" I asked.

"You will stay in a safe house with a police guard. You will not know where you are, but we will drive you there and back here again very early in the morning. The meeting with Mr Bonham and Credit Union de Paris is scheduled for 9:00 a.m. sharp."

The arrangement sounded agreeable. I would have slept on the station floor for all I cared; I was a free man! All three men left the room, and I took the opportunity to call Nancy. With some hesitation, I dialled.

"Hello," came the warm, soothing sound of Nancy's voice.

"Hi Nancy, how are you darling? I can't believe it—I'm actually free!"

"Josh, I don't understand what's happening. When I heard the news yesterday on TV that a fugitive had been shot, I was in shock, and I instantly went to the police. They reassured me everything was okay and mentioned there might be a killer at large and that you were still in danger. They also said I must be kept in a safe house, so last night I was in South London somewhere. In fact, I'm still here now."

"I'm so sorry about the mess Nancy. I didn't think it'd come to this. But all is good now; I'm with the French police, also in protection."

"They can't say any more at this stage. The safe house was unfortunately a necessary precaution because I had your mobile phone. They suspect it could have been tracked by the fraudster," Nancy explained.

"That's true, who has my phone now?"

"The police. When are you coming back?"

"I don't know yet. They need my help on something tomorrow. There is a chance they can catch the person who poisoned Mr Bertrand."

"I really hope they do. We need to get back to normal and prepare for the wedding!"

I closed my eyes. "I love you darling, I have to go now."

"I love you too!"

Relieved that Nancy was safe, I got up and went to the lounge area opposite for a refreshment. A sign outside stated it was strictly for witnesses and civilian visitors. The TV was showing the main news stories, and I perched on a sofa facing it. Yesterday's shooting did not feature at all. I had the lounge all to myself for around thirty minutes, but then the door opened. I couldn't be bothered to turn around to see who it was, however, whoever had entered recognised me instantly.

"Mr Rosenburg?" a man's voice exclaimed.

I turned to greet whoever had called my name and was stunned when I saw the thin man whom I'd met in the luggage compartment on the Eurostar.

"What the hell are you doing here? I thought you'd be in Italy by now?" I asked with a smile that normally greats an old acquaintance.

"Well, I am on the witness protection program now!"

"What?"

"So, the moment we got off the Eurostar, I was followed."

"Sounds familiar," I said under my breath.

"I was followed by some nasty people; they took all my possessions and threatened me." His comments got me nervous, I hope I hadn't implicated this man in my fraud case. "These people were human traffickers. They make their living by taking people against their will from other countries to the UK. Really evil people."

"What did they want with you?"

"They had spotted me on the train, not for the first time. I also had seen one of them before, someone I had met on the train six months ago, obviously in the luggage department!"

"Obviously!" I agreed with a grin.

"They knew I could evade the authorities with ease, and they wanted me to help them, you know, take some people to England. They threatened to report me to the authorities if I didn't help and held on to my possessions. So I escaped, without any money, possessions or ID, and also without your Rolex! They stole it!"

I winced at the thought of prized Rolex gracing the wrist of some unsavoury criminal. "Don't worry about that. I'm sorry to hear all this."

"I wandered the streets for the next few days, not knowing what to do. Then I got thinking. I was tired of running from one place to the next. I was tired of not having a home, changing my identity every few years and even not knowing who I was. It all got to me. I thought about settling down and stop pretending to be someone else. It was then that I went to the French police. I told them I knew the whereabouts of some traffickers; they were very interested in what I had to say."

"Good on you," I reassured.

"I also admitted to entering the country illegally and asked them to make me a deal. Initially, they were reluctant, but they were very impressed with my grasp of French, as I am not native you know."

"Your pronunciation is excellent."

"They liked the fact I had made the effort to learn their language so well, and they offered me immunity and a French residency visa if I could help them find the people smugglers. So I spent a couple of days helping build e-fit photos and showing them the hidden routes into the Eurostar."

At this point, the inspector entered the lounge and interrupted me. "Mr Rosenburg, please can we resume in 10 minutes. We need to go over the plan and then I have arrangements to make with Credit Union de Paris."

"Sure," I replied.

The thin man continued. "I am now on the witness protection programme. I live in the safe house, and we are pursuing the traffickers. One of them has been caught already and the police have rescued a 21-year-old woman as a result."

"That's really good work! You know I never got your proper name?"

"I am Lukas, Lukas Grigas. This is the real me. Originally I'm from Lithuania."

"Well Lukas, I wish you all the best for the future."

"It was nice meeting you again Mr Rosenburg. By the way—I feel really bad about your watch."

"The main thing is that you're in a very good place now."

"Thank you, take care."

Back in the interview room, the inspector then continued. "Have you understood what I have said so far?"

"Makes sense to me. But tell me, what did you make of the loan agreement?" I asked.

"When we found your laptop in the hotel room, we couldn't find any information on it. It was then that we contacted Omega Centurion Investments and their computer expert Hitesh."

"You spoke to Hitesh?" I exclaimed.

"Yes, he helped us with our enquiries and then confessed that he'd met you and that you both had uncovered some valuable information. He pleaded with us about your innocence and showed us all the data he had downloaded."

"Sorry about that, I didn't want to get him in any trouble," I said.

"Hitesh's evidence, together with Scotland Yard identifying the food inspector at the Eurostar terminal as the man in the restaurant video, changed the course of the investigation. We decided that if you were right, someone was definitely trying to steal money from Mr Bertrand other than you. The IOU arrangement did not seem strange as other banks confirmed that this type of transaction does happen. We started following the food inspector from the point where the train left Kings Cross station, who as it happens was following you!"

"How long was he following me?"

"On the Eurostar, the food inspector planned to get you arrested, but he had no idea you were posing as Mr Bonham; he thought you were Mr Rosenburg. That's why the announcements on the train referred to your proper name. Had you come forward, you'd have been arrested immediately. Also, you were quite lucky to bypass French passport control. From the video footage at Gard du Nord station, the food inspector was waiting for you to go through immigration like everyone else, but you didn't."

"That's right! As it happens, I have my friend who's in the lounge over there to thank for that."

"Oh, Lukas! Is that how you two know each other? What a small world," said the inspector. "However, I should add that you did a terrible job at remaining elusive!"

"It's not easy being on the run in a foreign city!" I replied, unreasonably stung.

"Once we arrested you the first time around and you escaped, it didn't take long for us to track your whereabouts. It was whilst following you to the Sacre Coeur that we came across the food inspector again. We were lucky to find you just in time before he held a gun to your head. The French police killed him as he was about to commit murder. By this time, we had established that your false identity had been unmasked by the real culprit, and he had no choice but to try to kill you. But you really messed up their plan."

"Thanks for saving me," I said gratefully. "Why was my death reported in the news rather than the food inspector?"

"That was a plot conjured up by the French police. We left your ID in his pocket, and the media reported that you had died. We barred them from publishing any photos. This way we hypothesised the real mastermind would think you were dead. Hopefully, now he might come forward and reveal his true identity."

"So as far as the mastermind is concerned, I'm dead and his accomplice has gone missing. So in order to get the money, it's likely he'll show up."

"Well, let's see what happens tomorrow. By the way—what made you pose as Mr Bonham, and where did you get your fake ID?"

"Well, I had a feeling that if Mr Bonham was behind this, he would have instructed his bank to transfer the repayment proceeds to an offshore account. The only way I could change the transfer details was to pose as him."

"Pretending to be Mr Bonham was highly risky and you could have easily been killed," said the inspector. I sat there contemplating the sequence of events. There were too many 'what ifs' and things could have turned out so wrong.

"And getting the fake ID?" he pressed.

"I got it at a place very close to where I live."

Inspector Renee then smiled. "Ah the place on Page Street, London. We've been monitoring it for quite a while. They're a cocky bunch! By the way, we hypothesise that the mastermind is Mr Bonham or someone who knows him. He has gone to great lengths to get his hands on this money. As you know, 'layering' is a technique that masks the original fraudulent transaction with subsequent bona fide transactions. So we think the initial IOU is counterfeit and will be legitimised by the loan repayment. Killing Mr Bertrand would be a clever way of removing any remaining evidence."

"That makes a lot of sense and what I suspected too," I said. "Why was the loan arrangement made on such a lengthy time scale?"

"We suspect the five year term of the IOU was created to give the fraudster sufficient time to carefully plan the murder of Mr Bertrand, it's been on the cards for some time."

"But what do we truly know about Mr Bonham? Is he the mastermind, a victim or genuine?" I enquired.

"Hmm…that is the tricky part. We know he was in the UK five years ago, but apart from a trip to the Cayman Islands, we really don't know his whereabouts."

"How did the food inspector know about Mr Bertrand's allergy?" asked Officer Du Pre.

"Good question," Inspector Renee said. "Mr Rosenburg, did you ever relay any personal client information about Mr Bertrand to anyone at Omega?"

"Yes, some, but only in the capacity as necessitated by the client meeting. Neither was I aware of Mr Bertrand's allergy nor did I inadvertently pass this information on by giving someone else access to the client's file."

"Do you think someone at Omega could have accessed Mr Bertrand's computer files?" Inspector Renee asked.

"That's a real possibility," I said. "Someone with the correct know-how could, with some difficulty, hack into the computer system, or access it themselves if they had the correct seniority and privileges."

"Yes, our analysis concludes the mastermind had access to both clients' files. The allergy would be the perfect way to commit a murder."

"So back to the plan tomorrow—where do I fit into this?"

Officer Du Pre then explained, "We know that the potential mastermind has a meeting with the bank at 9:00 a.m. There are a few outcomes. Firstly, if he is not the man in the photo, it should be clear to us he is an imposter. Most of these financial crimes happen over the phone and the internet, but in this case, we have the advantage of visual identification."

"Definitely," agreed Inspector Renee.

Officer Du Pre continued, "If criminals do use ID, it's normally their own photo on a fake document. We seriously doubt anyone would pose as someone else and attempt to mimic their physical appearance. Secondly, if the ID looks false or they can't complete the security questions, then we will have reason to arrest them. Lastly, we can't rule out that the real Mr Bonham will actually turn up. If that happens to be the case, then we do nothing. The bank has made it clear they do not want to risk any reputational damage or any resulting financial loss from a lawsuit."

"Ah, so there's one eventuality that could result in the fraud taking place under our noses," I said, "and that's if the real Mr Bonham turns up."

"Yes it is true," said the inspector. "Anyway, we need to be at the bank an hour earlier than the meeting time. You need to assist us to help identify the man purporting to be Mr Bonham."

"So the plan is for me to be at the bank with the police?"

"Yes, it's fairly simple," said Officer Du Pre. "We let the meeting go ahead as normal. All of us will be in a surveillance room next door monitoring events on a video conferencing unit, together with a psychologist. Given you are an expert in client service management, your task will be to examine everything about the meeting, the questions asked, anything to do with Omega Centurion or money transfers. You need to mention anything that looks abnormal or outside of standard procedure. All the client's replies need to be scrutinised for inconsistency. Do you understand?"

"Yes, and if I do spot anything, what happens then?"

"We will alert Sandrine, and she can start probing further to see if the replies all add up," replied Officer Du Pre.

"That sounds good. How well are Sandrine and the compliance officer at the bank prepared for this?" I asked.

"As far as they are concerned, it will be business as usual. They need to treat it as a normal client engagement, but they will ask additional security questions, given you have provided them with the perfect excuse to be cautious."

"Do I need to be undercover in any way?"

"No, you've played that part already!" said Inspector Renee with a sense of sarcasm.

"So, whether Mr Bonham is arrested at the bank, or not—when do I go home?"

"Good question again. If there is no arrest, the money transfer will happen. We can only take things further in light of new evidence, either from Omega or Mr Bertrand. Needless to say, if there is an arrest, you may be required for another day to give a statement and go over the information that Hitesh gave us," said Inspector Renee.

"Thank you, inspector. You have been a great help. I sincerely hope we catch this person tomorrow."

"Me too! Now, Officer Paul will take you to a safe house. You are to remain there and will be brought back here at 7:45 a.m. Then we'll make our way to the bank. For dinner this evening, you can speak to the guard at the safe house. Don't worry, we have a generous budget as we know you like fine cuisine!"

I laughed out loud. "Thanks for letting me finish breakfast this morning. You should go there sometime."

Inspector Renee smiled and said his goodbyes. I accompanied Officer Paul out of the station and we got into an unmarked car. The time was close to 6:00 p.m. The unmarked car drove through an area I recognised, Batignolles in the 17th Arrondissement. Once there, it wasn't long before I was at the safe house, a modern block of apartments about eight stories high. The officer summoned the lift and selected the top floor, inserting a key for it to register its ascent. When the doors opened, rather than seeing a long corridor which I expected, there was an open reception area with a guard sitting at a desk. The entire top floor was a dedicated protection facility.

"Bonsoir, I have Mr Rosenburg here for one night."

"Apartment 803," replied the guard.

Officer Paul then stretched out his hand to say goodbye. "Mr Rosenburg, there is a change of clothes in the apartment. Please wear them tomorrow."

"Thank you," I said, feeling a complete sense of relief and safety. I hadn't felt like this for days. I collected the room key and entered the apartment. It was functional and clean, with some great views towards Montmartre. I sat down and switched on the TV, contemplating where to order dinner.

Chapter 15
Operation Bee

An alarm call at 6:30 a.m. promptly woke me up. For the first 15 seconds of being awake, I felt dazed and didn't know where I was.

This was going to be a big day. It would determine whether Mr Bertrand was to be defrauded out of tens of millions or not. Maintaining this thought in my mind, I hurriedly got dressed. The guard had arranged a small breakfast at 7:00 a.m. sharp. It arrived on time, and I was ready to leave by 7:30 a.m.

I heard a knock on the door; it was Officer Paul again, and we departed for the station. When we arrived, I was taken to the same interview room as yesterday and told to wait.

Inspector Renee then burst in, but rather than initiating a greeting, he jumped on his radio. "Can all units commence Operation Bee? We are heading to the location, can all surveillance systems be readied!"

I felt an adrenaline rush. These people were relying on me and my expertise, I couldn't fail them. They needed me to help them but equally, I wanted to do justice for my client and friend.

After another five minutes on the radio, Inspector Renee finally turned to me. "Good morning Mr Rosenburg, are you ready? We'll leave in a couple of minutes."

"Yes," I replied, with a sense of exhilaration and nerves.

"Good. When we get to the bank, our surveillance team will set you up with an earpiece and microphone. Officers Paul and Du Pre will be with you all the time. The psychologist is due at the bank shortly."

"Understood," I said.

We left the room, taking the back entrance of the station into an unmarked van. Both officers were already inside.

"We need to go over some safety procedures," said Officer Du Pre as we left for the bank. "Under no circumstances must you leave our presence, and you must follow our instructions."

"Yes," was my terse reply. There was a lot to process.

The caller who had declared himself to Sandrine as the real Mr Bonham, sat in his hotel room in central Paris. He was reading a Monday journal, absorbed in an article appealing for witnesses in the Rosenburg murder case. There was a knock at the door; stepping slowly towards it, he looked through the door's spyhole. It was room service.

"Your chauffeur is here Mr Bonham. May I take any bags downstairs for you?"

"Morning," the man said. "No, that's fine. I've only got my briefcase."

After room service had left, the caller checked his phone. There were no messages, so he promptly went to the waiting taxi. "The Champs-Élysées please," he said, "I'll tell you when to stop."

"Yes, Monsieur."

The unmarked police van with me, Inspector Renee and the two officers made its way along the Champs-Élysées. Memories of marching up and down the avenue buying clothes and eating out while on the run sprang to mind; what a goose chase it had been. The van pulled up near the bank.

I got out with one of the officers, and we walked towards the back entrance, entering via a staff door. The other two soon followed five minutes later. We were taken to a conference room adjacent to the room where Mr Bonham was due.

I introduced myself to the psychologist, and we all sat down. Our room had four screens, one displaying the room next door from two hidden cameras. There was also another screen with all sorts of data outputs, a voice synthesiser, temperature and humidity display as well as a readout of the air quality in the room. The final two screens had views of the front and rear exits of the building.

"What's the air quality monitor for?" I asked.

Officer Du Pre replied: “We need to make sure there isn’t some sort of biohazard being brought into the room. We’ve seen it before!”

Officer Paul set me up with a microphone and hidden earpiece. “In an unlikely scenario where we get separated, you can contact the operations control room.” The instructions went on until there were only five minutes left before the meeting start time.

Over the video conference unit came the initial report. “We have sight of a man heading towards the entrance, he is not a staff member,” said the voice.

We all turned to the screen showing the front entrance. Instead of going straight into the bank, Mr Bonham stopped, stood outside, and lit a cigarette.

The psychologist was the first to comment. “If this is him and he is five minutes early, lighting a cigarette seems in keeping with the character profile we have. It is not something a criminal would do to attract extra attention right outside.”

I didn’t know what to make of it and remained glued to the screen. The man finished his cigarette at exactly 9:00 a.m. and then entered the bank, walking straight to reception. The front door camera swivelled around so we could get a clear view of his new position.

“Good morning. I have a meeting with Sandrine Levant at 9:00 a.m.,” said the man.

“Bonjour Mr Bonham, yes she’s expecting you. I’ll call her right away,” came the cheery reply from the bank receptionist.

In the surveillance room, Officer Paul spoke next. “Do we have a visual confirmation of Mr Bonham and the photos we have?”

“Negative, he’s too far away to get a proper visual. As well as a match in his appearance we are looking for a distinctive mole on the side of his face,” said the voice on the conference unit.

Mr Bonham waited; he seemed calm, at ease with his surroundings. He was typing away on his phone as Sandrine emerged from the lift and approached him.

“Mr Bonham?”

“Hello.”

“Nice to meet you. I’m Sandrine; please follow me.” He followed and Sandrine made polite chat about the weather that morning. “Come this way,” she indicated. They entered the meeting room.

In the surveillance room, we all watched eagerly as he entered. I did not recognise him, but he looked a similar age to Mr Bertrand. Everyone was focused on the screen showing the meeting room, which already had two occupants inside.

"Please take a seat—can I get you a drink?" Sandrine asked.

"No thank you."

"May I introduce my colleagues? This is Matthieu Le Bon from Compliance and Camille Chevre from Systems Security. Mr Bonham, you can appreciate that we need to cover some additional security questions in consideration of your call the other day. We sincerely apologise for the mishap on Saturday. Please rest assured that your account is frozen until the conclusion of this meeting."

Mr Bonham spoke in English but with a mild French accent. "Thank you for requesting that I attend in person to the branch. I had a real shock on Saturday when you mentioned someone had impersonated me. Especially since I am expecting some large flows on my account today. So I can see why the additional questions are required. I understand you're only doing your job," he said.

Back in the surveillance room, no one spoke. Nothing was alarming about how the meeting had started.

"We can go over the pending transactions in a moment. Did you bring all the paperwork?"

"Yes, I have it all here," said Mr Bonham, opening his briefcase.

"Firstly, please can you be so kind as to show us your passport and driving licence?"

"Certainly." He placed the items on the table in front of Camille, who immediately began inspecting them.

Over the conference unit, the Controller's voice sounded. "We are making visual identification right now, it all seems good. We have identified his facial features; he matches the photo evidence we have." My heart deflated. This was not how I'd played things out in my mind.

Sandrine returned to the questioning. "Can we now go over some account details, please? I see your account hasn't been used for a long time, except for a withdrawal last week."

"What! I wasn't aware of that!" cried Mr Bonham.

"Sorry sir, but the imposter who met me on Saturday withdrew 3,000 Euros." The officers sitting next to me stared in my direction, and I shook my head realising what I had done.

"That is outrageous!" exclaimed Mr Bonham. "What about any other transactions?"

"Luckily it was only 3,000 Euros. Rest assured Mr Bonham, everything else appears ok. We will make good the withdrawal—it was the same person who met me, we have validated that."

The Controller raised a question with the psychologist. "What do you think of his reaction to the 3,000 Euro withdrawal?"

"It seems genuine," she replied. Looking at her notes, the psychologist continued. "He was not aware of the withdrawal when he called Sandrine."

In the meeting room, Sandrine asked her next question. "But can I ask why there's been no activity on the account for so long?"

"To cut a long story short, I've been in England for the last five years, except for a trip to my new home in the Cayman Islands. Five years ago I went to the UK to arrange a few deals for several business acquaintances, one of whom was Mr Bertrand. Shortly after, I was involved in a car crash and got injured quite badly. It took years to recover; then my mother died, and I semi-retired. I haven't conducted much business since. I haven't been to France until this year." Officer Paul and Officer Du Pre looked at each other with a nod. It all seemed plausible.

"Sorry to hear that. Can you tell me more about the arrangements you have with Mr Bertrand, please?"

"Yes, well, I only have one open deal on my account, and that is about to be concluded. Alain needed to borrow 20 million for a business venture, and at the time I had the money to loan him, albeit at a decent interest rate for me. So we entered into a loan agreement. This is the deal that will be repaid today. I'm lucky I called on Saturday to make sure the arrangements were all fine."

When he finished, I spoke to the Controller overseeing the video conference. "What he says sounds believable, but there's something in the way he says it. I can't put my finger on it."

"Noted," said the Controller. "Anything from you, Inspector Renee?"

"No, it seems all very normal. Can someone validate his mother's date of death please? And the car crash, there must be a record."

"Okay," said the Controller.

Sandrine then asked: "Can you give me more details of the 20 million deal you mention."

"Certainly, here is the paperwork of the loan agreement, signed by a legal representative and Alain Bertrand."

"Thank you," said Sandrine. "Do you know Mr Bertrand is in hospital?"

"I had no idea! Is he okay?"

"I believe he is in a coma. His bank tried to contact him for some routine checks relating to this transaction, but obviously, he was unable to answer them. With your permission, may I call Omega Centurion as they want to verify the arrangement you have?"

"Certainly. I am sorry to hear about his situation."

The psychologist then interrupted the conference call. "His reaction shows genuine remorse and surprise." Inspector Renee agreed.

Meanwhile, Sandrine dialled Omega with the loudspeaker enabled. "Hello, can I speak to Bob Henderson, please?"

I heard Bob's familiar deep-voiced reply. "Bob speaking."

"Hello Bob, this is Sandrine from Credit Union de Paris. Regarding what we were discussing over email, I have Mr Bonham here to go over the details of the loan arrangement with Mr Bertrand."

"Hello Sandrine, hello Mr Bonham," Bob said. "I need you to answer a few questions. Mr Bertrand is not around and we've got some standard queries. Firstly, your investment account at Omega has not been touched for about five years, is that correct?"

"Yes, I invested in some of your funds when I first joined Omega but then cashed out my investments."

"Can you give me more details on the loan arrangement you had with Mr Bertrand?"

"Yes, as I explained to Sandrine, I lent him 20 million from one of my other bank accounts. We had agreed he would return the money with 4 million in interest from his investment account at Omega. I trust there are sufficient funds in his account to do so?"

"Yes, indeed there are," said Bob.

Sandrine interjected. "Bob, I've got a term sheet here and you should have one too, it details what was lent, when it is due to be repaid and all the signatures on it. The third-party witness is a law firm in France, as you will find on the document."

"Yes I can see, the paperwork is in good order and it's been double-checked," said Bob. "Mr Bonham, once the repayment occurs, would you like to reinvest the money back into your Omega investment account?"

"I may do so at a later date, but I need to transfer the money to another business colleague once it arrives."

"I see, that's all from me," said Bob.

"Thank you very much for your time," said Sandrine and terminated the call.

I had a sickening feeling that Mr Bonham was not going to give anything away. The discussion seemed genuine, the paperwork presented appeared to be correct; maybe it had been a wild goose chase after all.

The inspector turned to me. "Anything?"

"No, unfortunately, it all looks good. They've done more than what's required. But there is something in that man's voice; I swear it'll come to me," I said.

"Then we cannot arrest the man. Controller, can you replay the conversation with Bob again? Also, any word on his mother passing away?"

"Yes, inspector. We haven't validated the car crash, but his mother did pass away three years ago in Reims."

Sandrine continued. "Mr Bonham, can we turn to the transfer please. Where would you like the money deposited?"

"I need to transfer €25 million to a business colleague based in the British Virgin Islands. The repayment plus the one million Euros I had in the account already," said Mr Bonham.

"Do you have his details? Shall we revert to the details we had before Saturday?"

"Yes, it's the original transfer that had been arranged a few months back. The details are on this slip of paper." Sandrine typed away on her laptop. Mr Bonham's eyes wandered around the room. At one point, he stared directly at the concealed camera within a telephone unit.

At this point, Matthieu, who was sitting patiently beside Sandrine, stepped in. "To authorise the transaction, please can you give me characters one, four and seven from your passcode, and also can you write your signature here." Mr Bonham signed the paper that Matthieu had handed him, and he also provided the correct passcode responses.

"When would you like this money transferred?" Sandrine asked.

"I want it in my business colleague's account as soon as possible."

"Certainly," said Sandrine. "Can you give me a moment? I also need to check one last thing." She left the meeting room and jumped on her mobile phone.

The Controller announced that Sandrine was joining our conference call. "Is there anything we need to say to Sandrine? She says she is happy to go ahead and unfreeze the account," said the Controller.

In the surveillance room, I turned to both officers. "Can he not be arrested?"

"On what grounds?" said Officer Du Pre. "He seems like the genuine article, and from my perspective, you seem more culpable than him!" The psychologist also nodded in agreement.

"Oh, not this again," I moaned.

"At this point, there seems little doubt he is the correct Mr Bonham," said Inspector Renee. "However, we must tell Sandrine to continue. Controller, it's all good from our side."

Sandrine returned to the meeting room and tapped away at her laptop. "All is fine Mr Bonham, I'm just unfreezing your account. The transfer request will then be processed."

"Thank you for resolving the situation," said Mr Bonham. "I hope our mutual friend Alain Bertrand gets better. I need to go now, but feel free to call me on my mobile if you have any further queries?"

"Certainly," replied Sandrine. "We will also let you know when the reimbursement of the 3,000 Euros takes place, hopefully by tomorrow."

"Thank you again."

"Well, it was nice meeting you sir," said Sandrine, reaching out a hand. "Camille will show you out."

After wishing everyone a good day, he left the room. Sandrine immediately got on her mobile to the surveillance room. "I have no doubt he is the real Mr Bonham, and I don't think he's a fraudster."

"I agree," said Officer Du Pre. "The only fraud on this account has been conducted by our friend sitting right here."

I stopped and gave the officer a Machiavellian stare. "There's something in his voice that's very familiar, the vocal pitch," I said.

"What do you mean?" asked Inspector Renee, looking at the front view screen expecting Mr Bonham to emerge from the building any moment.

"Can we replay the scene where he talks about the loan agreement?"

"Sure," said the Controller. The screen promptly replayed the footage of the loan conversation for the third time.

"I've heard this man before, I promise you. Can we replay it one more time?"

I could hear someone sigh over the conference unit but my request was fulfilled. On the front view screen, we could see Mr Bonham emerge onto the Champs-Élysées and hail a taxi. I closed my eyes to focus on the voice of Mr Bonham, to remove the image of the face that was on screen. The more I listened, the more a horrible, nauseating thought came to my mind.

I opened my eyes. "It's Miles!"

"What? Miles who?" asked Officer Du Pre.

"Miles from Omega. That is Miles' voice but spoken in a French accent. He's wearing a face mask."

"How can you be so sure?"

I thought for a minute. "If it is Miles, surely he can't be at work? Phone Omega and see if he's there?"

"Do you want to do the honours?"

"Most certainly," I exclaimed. I phoned Stacey's number from the conference phone on the table.

"Hello, Omega Centurion," answered Stacey with a formal tone.

"Hi Stacey, it's Josh."

"Oh my god! We're not supposed to be talking to you," she cried.

"Stacey, I need an urgent favour. Is Miles in the office today?"

"I'm not sure whether I can divulge that information Josh."

"Look, trust me on this, it's very important."

"Er, well, no he's not, he's got today and Tuesday off," she replied.

"Thanks Stacey. Not a word to anyone else now—got to go, bye." I put down the receiver and breathed a sigh of relief. My hypothesis was beginning to look real. Ignoring the surveillance screens, I faced the officers in the room. "If I phone Miles' work number, he'll either pick up if it has been diverted to his mobile, or it'll go to voicemail. Either way, you'll have a sample of his voice to compare to Mr Bonham's."

Inspector Renee leapt up from his chair. "Controller, don't lose sight of Mr Bonham's taxi!" he shouted, and then turning to me, "phone him, phone him now!"

The phone rang; as I had guessed, it went to voicemail. "This is Miles Cooper; I'm not around at the moment but please leave a message."

"Controller, did you get a sample of the message?" asked Inspector Renee.

"Yes sir," came a swift reply.

"And does it match the voice of Mr Bonham?"

"We're just checking now." We waited about a minute or so. "Sir, it's a very close match! But we don't have a long enough sample to be 100% sure."

"I'm sure it's Miles!" I repeated.

"Controller, please relay the position of Mr Bonham's taxi, we will make chase!" yelled the inspector. "Quick, back to the van."

We scrambled out of the surveillance room and into the lift. "We can stop the transfer payment, but I'm not sure we'll get hold of Mr Bonham," said Officer Du Pre.

Officer Paul called the Controller. "Hello guys, are you tailing Mr Bonham?"

"Yes, his taxi is heading towards the La Défense district. There's quite a bit of traffic."

"Understood, keep his position, we are going to follow behind."

The unmarked police van was waiting for us at the back entrance. As we drove towards the coordinates being relayed by the Controller, he made an announcement. "The taxi is coming to a stop; it's at a hotel, the Pullman."

The driver of the police van took note and adjusted his route. "How does Miles know Mr Bertrand?" asked Officer Du Pre.

"Miles has been at the firm for over 15 years. He definitely knows Mr Bertrand, and most probably the real Mr Bonham."

"If your theory is right, do you think he might have killed Mr Bonham?"

"Yes possibly," I replied. "It's worth looking into Mr Bonham's details a lot closer."

"Definitely," said Officer Du Pre.

"Has anyone contacted Sandrine?" asked Inspector Renee, inadvertently sticking his elbow into my rib as the van sped through a red light.

"Yes," said the Controller. "I'm told the transfer has been frozen again. By the way, there is no activity from the hotel."

"Do we have a photo of the real Miles?"

"No," said the inspector. "Keep monitoring; we have Mr Rosenburg here to confirm a visual. Will be there in one minute."

"Understood," said the Controller. "We'll circulate the photo as soon as we have it."

The hotel was based in a wider compound of modern buildings that form the La Défense complex. There were long stretches of pedestrianised walkways adjoining tall buildings and office blocks. Wide roads with service lanes branched off into car parks, delivery entrances and overpasses. Searching for someone here was not going to be easy, but at least traffic was relatively thin.

The police van screeched to a halt outside the hotel. Both officers ran towards it, armed and scuffling past a group of people who had emerged from the revolving doors.

Once inside, Officer Du Pre went straight to the front desk while Officer Paul stood by the lifts.

"Morning, I'm Officer Du Pre. We are chasing a suspect, and we believe he is in the hotel. Police vans are covering the surrounding area of the hotel. Please close all the doors, no one is to leave or enter the building," he instructed.

"Certainly officer." Other staff at the front desk overheard the conversation and immediately alerted security.

"We are looking for a Mr Bonham. Has he checked into the hotel?"

"Let me look, sir. Well yes, he's in room 910 on the 9th floor." Both officers began ascending the building, one in the lift and the other up the staircase.

"We've locked down the hotel. Can all police units check the nearby vicinity?" instructed the Controller.

"Time to go," said Inspector Renee to the driver. "We need to scan the outside of the building." Conscious that both his officers were still in the hotel, he turned to me, "Please follow my instructions; you look on the left and I'll do so on the right."

The police van crawled along Rue Michel Ange, immediately outside the hotel. It got to a mini-roundabout and the driver took the first exit, with the hotel still on our left-hand side. Scanning constantly on my side of the van, I saw a few office workers taking a cigarette break.

The Controller spoke again. "All units should now have a photo image of the chief suspect. We are looking for someone matching this image or the person known as Mr Bonham."

Inspector Renee glimpsed at the photo on his phone. I looked at it too. It was surreal to think my client meeting had come to this. Looking at that photo brought back memories of the snide comments and derogatory remarks this man used to make. He was going to pay for this.

Out of nowhere, a car began approaching the van from the opposite side. Our driver ordered it to stop. Inspector Renee jumped out to speak to the driver and check the boot.

"Nothing," he said quickly returning. The van continued and we drove past a long line of motorbikes, all of which had dedicated pavement parking. I noticed a couple of men attending to their vehicles.

One of them was a small man, crouching, chaining his bike to a post. The other was walking, adjusting his helmet with the visor still open, ready to mount one of the bikes. It wasn't his face that caught my eye, but his stature and walk.

The brain is fascinating when it comes to human recognition. I had seen that walk; I recognised the stocky build of the man, and his height appeared to be correct. I was sure it was Miles!

"It's him!" I shouted, "there!" Our driver reversed the van to get closer to the man, who calmly flipped his visor down and started his bike.

"You sure?" came a knee-jerk reply from the inspector.

"I didn't see his face, but I know it's him," I replied.

At this moment, I couldn't resist, I opened my side of the window and shouted, "Miles!" The inspector looked at me in shock as the man turned his head momentarily. I couldn't see his face, but I was pretty sure it was him.

"Please, you need to follow my instructions," pleaded the inspector, relieved that I had found Miles but annoyed with my recklessness. "We have a visual on Avenue de l'Arche. A man on a motorbike. Black clothes and a black helmet. All units keep monitoring the hotel area just in case it isn't him."

The motorbike sped off, and another chase was about to commence. Meanwhile, we heard Officer Du Pre speak over the audio. "We have searched the hotel room where Mr Bonham was staying. It has been vacated. We can't find any mask or bodysuit. We'll continue looking."

There was no time to pick up the officers back at the hotel. The van's siren began to sound as it attempted to keep up with a much faster bike. The motorcyclist sped along Avenue de l'Arche and took a sharp right into Rue Berthelot. The van's engine must have been supercharged as I witnessed a speed and acceleration not possible for a vehicle of this size. However, its cornering ability didn't match its engine upgrade and the van precariously balanced on two wheels whilst negotiating the same corner as the bike. We both crossed a mini roundabout, the vehicles heading towards one of the main roads leading out of the La Défense area. In front of us was a junction with a tramline crossing our path. The bike went over the crossing at close to ninety miles per hour, and we followed, ignorant of any tram that might have emerged from either side.

The bike was now covering distance a lot faster than the van. Other police units were alerted to the chase and started descending on the surrounding roads.

"Controller, can we have a helicopter scan the University area, please?" requested Inspector Renee.

"We are monitoring the area," replied the Controller.

The motorcyclist turned left into Rue de Normandie and the police van lost sight of it for almost 20 seconds. It wasn't clear whether he was following a planned route or driving in a haphazard direction to avoid detection, but at the top of the road the motorbike turned left in the direction of the tramline again; it was now clear the latter appeared to be the case. Both vehicles crossed the tramline again, our van clearing the tracks as a tram approached.

We were now on Rue des Fauvelles, a long road that gave the motorbike a significant advantage. As much as our driver tried to push the engine to its maximum, the police van was too slow. By the time it had got to a V-shaped junction, we were not aware in which direction the motorcyclist had gone.

"Damn," shouted Inspector Renee. The driver looked blankly at us for the next instruction. "Wait here," said the inspector. Doubt, as well as a sinking feeling, began to creep within me. Was it even Miles on the bike? We hadn't seen his face. My confidence at the initial sighting was now diminished.

The Controller interrupted. "One of our vans blocking 'Avenue de Verdun' saw a motorbike conduct a U-turn down Rue Jules Ferry. Inspector Renee, you should have a visual of the suspect in 30 seconds."

Sure enough, we saw the bike speeding towards us; however, it was aware we were blocking the road. The van driver remained stationary, like a goalkeeper, trying to gauge in which direction an oncoming player might shoot. The motorbike braked furiously about 150 metres ahead, attempting to turn right at the same time. As it did so the rear wheel skidded enough for it to fall onto its side, with the rider still seated but lying horizontally.

The van remained stationary as our driver subconsciously gave the motorcyclist the courtesy to get to his feet and dust himself off. The motorcyclist, with his back facing us, quickly turned around and fired a gun. The bullet smashed through the reinforced windscreen and being a police vehicle, the glass did an incredible job of remaining intact except for a cherry-sized hole where the bullet had made contact.

This betrayal of the kind gesture our driver had afforded the rider annoyed him greatly. He slammed on the accelerator so hard that I got a stomach-turning feeling that most rollercoasters would love to emulate. We sped towards the bike. I don't think our driver cared whether we hit it at a fatal speed.

However, the motorcyclist appeared to only have suffered minor injuries and sprang back onto the bike, quickly resuming his getaway by turning into a road on our left. The chase was back on; whoever this person was, Miles or not, he was adamant not to get caught. After a short straight, the bike turned left again, and then another straight run ended with a swift right turn.

Our van was mimicking each move. The motorcyclist was injured because the bike was not shifting as fast as before. As the bike and van weaved through the streets of Paris and then onto a dual carriageway, I could hear a police helicopter hovering above.

The Controller got back on the microphone. “The helicopter is now tracking the suspect; he is heading towards the river. All units close in on the Les Guillaraies vicinity. Also, we have found a face mask and bodysuit in one of the service elevators at the Pullman hotel.”

Our van driver was keeping up the chase superbly, even discounting the advantage given to us by the helicopter. The motorcyclist was now very close to the river, with Parc du Chemin-de-l’ile on our right.

“I think we’ve got him,” exclaimed Inspector Renee. “Someone block off Boulevard de la Seine and Avenue de Hoche! The suspect can’t go further; the Seine is ahead, and he must turn around unless he takes the bike through the park.”

The motorcyclist approached the river, then realised that the roundabout ahead did not have any exits in a forward direction. He went around the roundabout twice as police vans blocked the only two escape routes that Inspector Renee had mentioned.

The bike then stopped, again facing us in another round of the duel. It raced forward and tried to turn into the park. However, its front wheel hit the kerb, resulting in the rider and his bike flying in the air, separating, and landing in different places.

“All police units, the suspect is now on his feet, but he is armed,” yelled the inspector into the microphone. “You stay in the van,” he said pointing his left hand at me while simultaneously opening the door with his right. I obeyed for a brief moment as Inspector Renee gave chase on foot, but feeling brazen, I also jumped out of the van, joining the pursuit.

The motorcyclist dashed into the park, in the direction of the A14 motorway, which hovered over the green space below. The inspector was 30 metres ahead of me and then I heard another shot. He dived to the ground as I hid behind some bushes, the bullet whistling past us both. Back on my feet, I ran and caught up with the inspector.

“I thought you said I wouldn’t be shot at today?” I joked with panting breath.

“Very funny, Monsieur.”

“What shall we do now?” I asked.

"We wait for the Controller to give us an update. The helicopter is locking his position."

"Move forward, he is taking a path towards the overpass and river," came the instruction from the Controller.

Inspector Renee resumed the chase, but with his gun drawn. "Stay behind me and look after my back. There are many trees and bushes for him to hide." We slowly crept forward, not being shot was my highest priority right now. Could this be the Miles that I knew from the office? Being rude and insolent was one thing; being a fraudster and killer was another.

Above the motorway barriers, I could see two police snipers. We edged forward, following the instructions from the Controller who had a bird's eye view of the situation. However, the motorcyclist unexpectedly popped up in the foliage ahead and fired two more shots. The inspector shrieked as one of the bullets grazed his ear, blood pouring down the side of his face.

"I'm ok," he reassured me, wiping the blood with his forearm. The snipers retaliated, not knowing whether their target had been hit or not. Unfortunately, they got their answer quickly when the motorcyclist fired back towards the overpass.

"There's not much he can do from here," whispered the inspector, "unless he jumps into the river. But we have a police boat covering that side too."

We remained still, and it occurred to me that I was the only one without a gun! I had been irrational again. I was risking my life—for God's sake, I had to get married in a few weeks!

After a five-minute stand-off, the motorcyclist reappeared. This time, when he took aim it was accurate. The inspector got hit in the leg. "He's got me!" he cried, falling to the ground and grabbing his limb. "Take my gun. There's no way I can use it."

"I'm not that good with guns," I said.

"Just take it, you might need it! I'll be fine, you need to provide me with cover now. I can't walk."

I realised that if I moved too far from the inspector's position, he would be a sitting duck. I would need to remain in his presence. "Inspector Renee has been shot!" I shouted into my microphone. "He's okay but can't walk."

"Acknowledged," responded the Controller. "Snipers, please cover the inspector's position." I understood it was a game of wits now. I had to show I could control the situation. If I saw the motorcyclist, I had to fire the gun or be fired at.

"Stay in your places," said the Controller. "He is between you and the river. Face towards it and monitor everything in front of you." In the distance, I saw some movement. It was him and as predicted he was making his way to the Seine. Neither did I get a clear aim at the assailant, nor did I have the courage to pull the trigger. However, a police sniper also caught the movement. He sat on the motorway bridge and peered through his telescopic lens, the cross at its centre positioned on part of a foot that was visible through the thick foliage. Years of training had taught him to be as steady as a statue but lightning-fast on the trigger.

He couldn't see any other body part of the motorcyclist and fortunately for the sniper, the assailant was stationary long enough for him to take a shot. So he fired, judging the wind speed and trajectory perfectly as the bullet hit its target. Both Inspector Renee and I heard a yell as the Controller spoke once more. "We have a direct hit, he's been shot in the foot. All units press forward."

Inspector Renee then gestured to me. "You remain here," he said, primarily out of concern for my wellbeing. From the riverbank appeared Officer Du Pre; I could see him making short strides towards me, broken by ducking manoeuvres. Instinctively the motorcyclist got up, took a shot at the officer and then limped in a diagonal path towards the river, before hiding again. *Surely it was only a matter of minutes before this man got caught,* I thought.

Officer Du Pre made a short run and was now within twenty metres or so from the motorcyclist, who without noticing the officer's latest move, got up and resumed his pathetic attempt at reaching the river. Officer Du Pre then sprinted and dived at him, managing to push the assailant's body forcefully sideways and causing him to land awkwardly on the ground. Slightly concussed, the motorcyclist got up but was immediately downed by Officer Paul who leapt for his legs with a well-rehearsed rugby tackle. It was safe for me to move forward. With the motorcyclist laying flat on the ground, Officer Du Pre stood a couple of metres away, pointing his gun at the assailant.

"Monsieur, you are under arrest!" The chase was finally over. The closer I got to the motorcyclist the more familiar his outline looked. The width of the shoulders and the size of his torso in relation to his legs.

"Miles, it's you isn't it?" I shouted.

There was no reply from the motorcyclist and Officer Paul asked: "Shall I open his visor?" This was the moment of truth.

"Yes," I said. The visor was pulled back; I saw enough of the face to know it was definitely Miles. I stared at his face, but his eyes were fixated on the ground.

All at once, I was furious. "How could you do this Miles? Think about the lives you've ruined—Mr Bertrand is still in a coma!" I yelled. "How could you betray David Highfield? He placed a lot of trust in you!"

"Mr Bertrand is an overprivileged buffoon!" Miles said.

"He may be from a very rich family, but he's a genuinely decent man. He donates generously every year to Omega's charities. Was it worth it? The plan to take 24 million?"

Miles winced in pain and didn't say anything, his eyes closed for a second as he held his foot.

"I could have been jailed because of you, you damn idiot!"

Again, Miles said nothing. The realisation that his five-year plan had failed seemed too much for him to bear. Officer Du Pre handcuffed him and then both officers picked him up and dragged him into the van.

I walked back to Inspector Renee, who was now being treated by medical staff. "I guess you want this back," I said, handing him the gun.

"Good work, Mr Rosenburg. I don't think we'd have got here without you."

"Well, I had to clear my name. It's been a very strange week to say the least!"

I was told to go back to the safe house in a separate police car and then report to the station at 4:00 p.m. I left with another officer who I had not seen before. On the way back to the safe house, it was only natural to mull over the events of the chase, although I didn't want to think about Miles and the fraud.

There were so many moments when it could have gone wrong, but it had ended well, albeit with Inspector Renee injured. I knew it was going to be a tense return to Omega. Fraud on this scale would have major implications for the Compliance team and the Financial Regulation bodies. I'm sure the entire company would be under scrutiny by the regulators, clients and staff.

Arriving at the safe house, I placed my lunch order with the guard at reception and counted down the time to return to the police station.

Chapter 16
The Explanation

When I arrived at the police station, the front desk mentioned that an urgent conference call with Scotland Yard had been scheduled, and I was told to wait in the station's lounge. Ten minutes later Officer Du Pre entered.

"Afternoon, Mr Rosenburg."

"Hi officer. How is Inspector Renee?"

"He's doing well; been taken to a military hospital, but he should be back home tomorrow evening. I will run the conference call with Scotland Yard, it's with Detective Chief Inspector Hardcastle. I take it you remember him?"

"Oh certainly. Hopefully, he'll see I was right after all!"

"Shall we go to the interview room now?" I followed the inspector to the room and we sat down, the conference screen was switched off. Officer Paul was already sitting inside.

"Mr Rosenburg, before we start can I make a small request?" asked Officer Du Pre. I nodded. "The 3,000 Euros you withdrew from Mr Bonham's account—the bank would like it back as soon as possible!"

"Most definitely! I was not intending to keep it—it was part of my plan."

"I understand, but the bank wanted to press charges until I explained you were involved in the operation. So they agreed to drop the charges and forfeit the interest due, but they want the original sum returned."

"They've got a cheek!" I said, but then thinking about what I had done, it was the best possible outcome. "Yes, I'll make the transfer after this meeting."

"How much do you have left?"

"Around 500 Euros," I said, red-faced.

"Fine dining is not cheap!" The officer quipped. "Please make sure you pay the full amount back to this account number and sort code," he said, handing me a paper slip.

Officer Paul then spoke. "By the way, good work Mr Rosenburg. Your help today was absolutely critical."

"He gave a good chase," I said.

"Well, he couldn't have got away from me," said Officer Paul. "Rugby tackles are my trademark." We all chuckled.

"I'm sure you got a lot of help from the sniper!" Officer Du Pre added. "Now let's see what Inspector Hardcastle has to say." He switched on the conference unit and the inspector popped up on the screen.

"Afternoon gentlemen," came a warm greeting.

"Hello inspector," I replied.

"Hello Mr Rosenburg, thanks for attending. There are a few pieces of the puzzle that we still need to fit together," Inspector Hardcastle said. "But first of all, I'd like to say congratulations on a job well done, particularly you Mr Rosenburg, not least because you were the forerunner in our enquiries not so long ago. But I'd like to start by confirming that Scotland Yard has formally charged Miles Cooper for the attempted murder of Mr Alain Bertrand and fraudulent activities at Omega Centurion Investments. There is an open question as to what has happened to the real Mr Bonham; unfortunately, we suspect foul play in his disappearance five years ago. We believe Miles had an accomplice to administer his crime, this person is still yet unidentified but who we know as 'the food inspector'. To clarify, he was the man shot dead by French police near the Sacre Coeur Montmartre. Scotland Yard has gone through the video footage at the Golden Orchid and the police conclude the food inspector was close enough to the food preparation area to dispense the poison. From all the witness statements and evidence gathered, we see him asking questions about the dishes and which table ordered them. We suspect that he slipped poison into Mr Bertrand's starter as he questioned kitchen staff and caused a distraction. But to repeat, it is not crystal clear from the video footage."

"That's really cunning," I said.

"We believe the timing of the food inspector's arrival at the Golden Orchid was not a coincidence. Miles Cooper was also invited to the luncheon meeting and knew perfectly well that Mr Bertrand would be there, providing a perfect opportunity to carry out the attempted murder without him being at the crime scene. Unfortunately for you Mr Rosenburg, the most likely suspect would end up being you!"

"Do you think he was trying to make it look like an accident?"

"Yes, we think so. One mistake the food inspector made was to apply too much of the poison to the dish. Even with a reasonable concentration, an amount equal to that naturally occurring on a food preparation surface, there would have been enough of it to affect someone in the same way that happened. It was this higher dose that alerted our forensics team to suspect foul play rather than an accidental cause."

"Have you found the poison yet?" enquired Officer Du Pre.

"No, but once we have the identity of the food inspector, we can then track his whereabouts and the places he visited."

"Mr Rosenburg, right from the outset it was hard for us to believe you could be the culprit. From all the character references and information we had on you, it did not add up—but we couldn't take any chances and had to follow procedure, so sorry about that." He paused. "We are still examining the loan agreement but as much as it looks genuine to all parties, we believe it is false. We suspect, and as you have concluded, the initial payment of 20 million was fictitious. We can't prove it yet until we have access to all of Mr Bonham's bank accounts; some of them are offshore. In the coming days, we may require your help on this point but also to understand more about Mr Bonham's relationship with Omega, which, unfortunately, seems to have ended due to nefarious actions by Miles Cooper."

"Do you think there were any other accomplices apart from the food inspector?" asked Officer Du Pre.

"Scotland Yard is checking with the help of the computer expert at Omega. The compliance team is going over the false payment instructions as we speak, but it all points to Miles Cooper falsifying documents which others had no reason to question."

"I suspect Miles made a respectable living being one of the senior traders. Why would he want to commit the fraud?" asked Officer Du Pre.

"Greed is always a primary factor, whether the perpetrator is rich or poor, but we are looking into his financial affairs. The compliance officer mentioned that Miles had reported some huge losses on technology stocks during the dot-com crash in the late nineties. One thing we do know is that the plan was constructed over a long period of time."

"Yes," interjected Officer Du Pre. "The face mask and bodysuit to mimic Mr Bonham would have required significant time to manufacture and required a good knowledge of his physical measurements and facial features. This is why we suspect Miles Cooper had something to do with his disappearance. Having a dead body is a convenient way of obtaining all the body measurements and photos one requires."

"It's shocking that he was planning this heinous crime all that time, and what you said about Mr Bonham makes sense. I can see how the loan agreement was a clever method of taking money from someone else's account and making it appear legitimate," said Officer Paul.

"Yes, an elaborate scheme that almost worked," said Inspector Hardcastle. "Josh, if you hadn't noticed that it was Miles at the meeting earlier this morning, we would have been incorrectly chasing the real Mr Bonham, wherever he is. What I mentioned earlier is also true—the toxin in the food could simply have led the investigation in a totally incorrect direction with the outcome being accidental poisoning. In that case, the restaurant owner would have been tried for manslaughter. Anyway gentlemen, I've taken up a lot of your time and there are many things to follow up on. No doubt I'll be in touch soon and once again, well done!"

"Is Mr Bertrand still in a coma?" I asked.

"No, but he remains under sedation and needless to say he can't talk," Inspector Hardcastle confirmed. "It's hard to get a proper update as the French Embassy is guarding him very closely."

"At least him being out of a coma is some welcome news," I said. "But I guess he's still got a long way to go."

"We'll speak soon as more information is uncovered," said Inspector Hardcastle. "One more thing—Mr Rosenburg, your fiancée is on her way to Paris, courtesy of the French police! She's arriving at Hotel de Bourbon soon."

"Oh, that's fantastic, thank you." We said our goodbyes and the call ended.

Officer Du Pre turned to me. "Nice to hear our friend's condition is improving. We have been under huge pressure to resolve this case." He paused for a second, mindful that he was about to give me more information than he should to a UK civilian. "I mean—Mr Bertrand's wellbeing is important to some very high-profile people."

"Yes, I gathered that from the beginning," I said.

"One final thing—you can have these back," he said, handing me my passport and driving licence. "And as for these," holding up the fake ID of Mr Bonham, "you'll need them to get back to the UK. Inspector Hardcastle will explain later."

I looked at the passports in his hand and shook my head. "Identity fraud is big business these days! But officer, you mustn't mention me at all in your investigations regarding the fake ID manufacturers. I was threatened with a gun. I actually live quite close to them."

"Don't worry; we have quite a large dossier of evidence on those people. They are getting too cocky. One of them is an IT guru, and she hacks into one of our databases quite regularly. We are trying to work out how she does it—that's why we've left their operation open."

"Well, I'm glad they were open for business when I wanted some ID." We both laughed.

When I left the police station, it was very late in the afternoon. Outside in the open air, I felt a mix of emotions; relief the nightmare was over, but anguish at the misery and upheaval that had been caused. Plus, there was the open question of Mr Bonham. Could there be more charges to be brought against Miles? Most probably.

The warm Parisian afternoon was an undisputable invitation to take a walk, to appreciate the surroundings and generally ponder life. Besides, I had plenty of time to get to Hotel de Bourbon, and after the hectic van chase earlier, I felt far more stable on two feet. Naturally, I thought about the events of the last week; it would be one of those stories to be told time and time again in finance companies around the globe. A deeper introspection of the entire investment community would be spawned at the highest levels of political office. It was the perfect opportunity for financial regulators to say, "I told you so," and wrap their regulatory tentacles further around the body of an injured investment community. I was sure the rules for client services management and my job at Omega would change forever.

Walking along the Champs-Élysées, there was no need to nervously watch over my shoulder, or twitch at the first person who caught my eye for longer than a few seconds. However, I was still getting used to my new state of freedom, and it was hard to absorb the scale of treachery that had gone on. I knew Miles was a nasty piece of work, but attempting to kill Omega's most respected client and then trying to shoulder the blame on me or the Golden Orchid was unimaginable. As I carried on my journey, I passed pavement cafés with diners inspecting menus and eating leisurely. I watched shoppers flitting from store to store making choices about what to buy. Then it dawned upon me; without taking the risks I had taken, I may not have been a free man to enjoy the simple things we take for granted every day. However, the sight of people calmly going about their pursuits in the surrounding boutiques and chic restaurants provided a good source of distraction. Soon I was at Place de la Concorde, facing the Jardin de Tuileries, a grand park with Hotel de Bourbon to my left. Suddenly, my phone rang, it was Henry. Rather than go straight to the hotel, I decided to take a detour through the park.

"How are you, my dear fellow?" I greeted.

"You sound more like your convivial self, I take it you're not a man on the run anymore."

"No, it's a long story, one which you won't believe, but I'll tell you properly when I'm back."

"Nancy called me from the Eurostar, apparently you helped the French police catch the fraudster at your company."

"It's all a bit hush at the moment, but yes. Thanks for helping out by the way."

"No worries. Well, glad to hear you are ok, can't wait to catch up over a drink," Henry finished.

"I'll see you in London."

By now, I was halfway through the park and gathered I should go directly to the hotel. The well-tended flowers beds had given me an idea; I had to apologise to Nancy somehow, so I stopped off at a florist outside the park and purchased a bouquet of pink roses. Strolling under the imposing arches that make up the facade of the buildings overlooking the park, I arrived at the hotel five minutes later.

"May I help you, sir?" asked the lady at the reception desk. She was the one who'd seen me arrested the previous day, but taking a good look at me she did not appear shocked. "Mr Bonham? Or is it Mr Rosenburg?" she smirked. "Don't worry, I had a call from Inspector Renee, he explained that you were helping French police, and as a favour, they have given you a complimentary two-night stay…with breakfast, I should add!" We both chuckled.

"That is very kind of the inspector. Has my fiancée arrived?"

"Yes, she has, I'll call her to let her know you're here. The room is on the sixth floor, here's another key. Shall I get the porter to assist you in any way?"

"No thank you, I'll find my way to the room. Also, I'd like to book 'La Salle de Bal' for dinner this evening for two people, say 8 o'clock?"

"Most certainly sir."

I arrived on the sixth floor and knocked on the door. To my immense satisfaction, I saw Nancy open it; she just stood there, and it gave me time to admire her warm smile and new outfit. Then we hugged, and I gave her a kiss.

"I'm so sorry to put you through all this darling. I had to prove my innocence." I handed over the bouquet.

"You did it, Josh. I can't believe you did it! If you hadn't done your own investigation, maybe there could have been a grave miscarriage of justice?"

"I can't believe it was Miles," I said.

"Miles!" she cried. "The trader chap that you've mentioned at work?"

"Yes, I still can't believe it was him. God, I'll be glad to get back to the office and tell everyone what a scoundrel and a cheat he is."

"When your name appeared on the news, everyone was phoning me, Josh. It was awful."

"Don't worry dear, it's all over. Did you phone my mother? I haven't had a proper chance to do so."

"I told her all is well."

We went into the apartment and sat down. The French police must have been grateful for my assistance as they had accommodated us in a signature suite. "Gosh, this is nice. Sure beats the safe house."

"It's such a magical place," said Nancy, looking out of the window towards an illuminated Eiffel Tower. "You're the most perfect man."

"And you, my dear are the most perfect woman, and we are getting married very soon!" I praised her for being so understanding and finished off by complimenting her shoes!

"Oh, I got them from a place in Chelsea, this boutique is new, exclusive…." She had begun describing the shop and how much Chela liked her choice. Life was back to normal…

Nancy had brought me a change of clothes, and we sat down for a long while having a chat, although I spared her a few of the scarier details such as the gun being pointed at my head. After a relaxing bath, we were ready for dinner. "I've got a good idea about the place you're taking me tonight, is it the restaurant downstairs?"

"Indeed it is my love. Are you ready?"

"Yes," she said.

We entered the restaurant and were greeted by the same maître'd who had served me yesterday. "Mr Bonham, nice to see you again," he said.

"Er, the name's Mr Rosenburg. I have a reservation at eight."

"Yes…Mr…please follow me," he said with a perplexed expression. I looked at Nancy, and she tried to contain her giggles. We sat down and were presented with the wine menu. I decided that champagne was in order and purchased a well-deserved bottle of '85 Krug. Nancy chose a langoustine and caviar starter, and I had asparagus with crayfish.

"Why did Miles try and pin it on you?" Nancy asked.

"I don't think he was after me personally; I happened to be in the wrong place at the wrong time. Mr Bertrand was my client, and it coincidently happened that the poisoning took place during my lunch meeting. I guess the police were looking to find any reason or cause and presumed my financial position was a possible motive."

"They were only doing their job," she said. "In our flat, when Inspector Hardcastle first said it could be poisoning, I didn't believe it whatsoever. It sounded preposterous, but after what you have told me, I can see how it was all plausible. Which hotel did you stay in by the way?"

"Darling, I was a hunted man, I stayed in a different hotel each night, I didn't even get to stay here although I'd checked in!" She laughed. I could now look at events with a sense of humour. "Oh, I even bumped into an old friend on my adventure. Do you remember James?"

"Briefly," she said. "Luck was definitely on your side. Look at it this way; as a result, we're in Paris for a few days. How romantic!" The logic of that comment did not tally up, and I was too thrilled to examine it further.

When the main dishes arrived the conversation fell silent for a while as we savoured the simple, divine flavours.

"Are you going to work on Thursday? The return ticket I have is for an evening train on Wednesday."

"I guess so, David may give me a few days off, but I'm keen to go in and explain a few things to reassure everyone. The company is exposed to reputational damage from media articles. They'll want to issue a statement."

"I see, so let's make the most of our trip!"

"Yes darling. One thing is for sure, Miles won't be missed at the office."

"It's shocking what people do for money!" Nancy stated.

"I know, but attempted murder is an extreme act. He'll be all over the papers in the coming days! Talking of people in the papers, the Chelsea Manager is a real star!" I said.

"Yes, I heard he's made a brilliant start since taking charge."

"Oh, I wasn't talking about the football. You know I invested a lot of money in Drenchin' Doughnuts?"

"Yes darling, how could I forget? How much are your losses now? Wasn't that the stupid place where someone slipped on a doughnut and claimed damages!" I started laughing out loud but then stopped. My mind pictured Mr Bertrand laughing at the same thing before the unfortunate incident.

"Yes, but I've made a small fortune on my investment!"

"You have?" queried Nancy, not absorbing what I had said. "How's that connected to the football manager?"

"Well, the Chelsea Manager went there with a few journalists. He loved the place! And they mentioned it on the sports pages! Now it's going to be bought out!"

"That's good news, you can take me there sometime!"

We decided to skip coffee, opting to have it later depending on wherever we went afterwards. Nancy insisted on paying for the meal, as a treat for all my hard work, so I let her. We left the restaurant and hailed a taxi outside.

"Where to, Monsieur?"

"Take us to Fontaine du Châtelet, *s'il vous plait*," I requested. The driver dropped us off by the fountain, and we took a long walk along the Seine. Memories of our courtship came flooding back and we relived the dreams we had dreamt as people newly in love. It was the best possible way to end such a day.

Chapter 17
Favour Required

The following morning we woke up uncharacteristically late. I had not received any further communication from the police, so it was going to be a day dedicated to exploring the city and shopping. The exhaustion from the big chase yesterday had left me with sore muscles and a bruised rib. Not having enough energy to get dressed for breakfast, we decided to have it sent to our room instead.

"It'd be nice to go to the Louvre—at school we've been studying sculpture. I showed the children a picture of the 'Winged Victory of Samothrace' the other day."

"Oh, what did the kids say?"

"Why hasn't it got a head?" Nancy laughed.

"Yes, the Louvre, lovely idea! What then?"

"I was thinking shopping on Rue du Faubourg Saint-Honoré and Avenue Montaigne, they're a short walk from here," Nancy replied.

"What a nice plan! Shall we go to the spa after that? My muscles are aching."

By the time we got dressed to go out, it was 11 o'clock. We decided to walk to the Louvre; Paris is that type of city, there's too much to take in and it's best done on foot.

After lunch, we were on track for a spot of haute couture shopping. We entered the first boutique, and I sat waiting patiently while Nancy tried on her third dress.

"What about this one?" she asked emerging from a booth.

"Nice, really nice. But the second one is my favourite."

"Hmm…let me try the other two that the sales assistant recommended," she said, and then disappeared back into the booth.

I continued to wait, looking at the messages on my phone that Nancy had returned to me yesterday. It rang all of a sudden.

"Mr Rosenburg?" enquired the caller.

"Yes, that's me."

"Oh, hello, this is Inspector Hardcastle. Hope you are well today?"

"Hi yes, relaxing today inspector."

"I bet, it was a hectic day yesterday. Look, we need your help again, but this time in London."

"I see." I closed my eyes.

"The mask and ID left at the Pullman hotel are being analysed. They hold the clues as to what happened to Mr Bonham. If we can establish where they were made, when they were made, we can gather more evidence and create a trail of events from that point in time. The fake passport alleging to be Mr Bonham and used by Miles Cooper was an excellent copy. If we can find its origin, that would be a fantastic lead. The thing is, we need an expert to look at it, one who may know where it was made; an expert who knows the murky world of operators that produce this stuff."

"Who would that be?"

"The ink used on the passport was from a different batch to the one that was used on yours, so we have concluded it wasn't the guy on Page Street. However, he may know who else is capable of producing such an item. We need you to make him a visit."

"But…but why can't the police do that?"

"There's a problem; they know we're tracking them. We sent one of our undercover officers there this morning, but they didn't open the door. They might have moved their operation. We don't want to raid them just yet. But you are known to them, they'll recognise you. You have a much better chance of speaking to them than anyone at Scotland Yard. Again…"

"One second, inspector," I requested, noticing Nancy had emerged from the booth, wearing dress number four.

"Blue looks gorgeous doesn't it?" She exclaimed.

"Yes darling. Although my favourite is still number two." She paused, looked at herself in the mirror and dived back into the booth.

"Please continue," I whispered into the phone.

"Again, it's about helping Mr Bertrand and the investigation. You are the right person to carry this through."

I contemplated the offer. I had come this far—it was only right that I help discover what happened to the real Mr Bonham.

"Okay," I replied. "When would you like me to do it?"

"The sooner the better; every day counts. Also, the French police and Scotland Yard would like to offer you a reward if you go ahead and assist us. We know you're putting yourself in danger because of our investigation."

"It's not about the reward for me; I need to get to the bottom of this on behalf of Omega. The company has treated me very well, and I should assist to ascertain what has happened to one of their clients."

"That's what I was hoping to hear. Don't worry Mr Rosenburg, we will have your back covered. As for the reward, it'll more than compensate you for your purchase of the fake ID!" I had completely forgotten my bank account was ten thousand pounds smaller since the visit to Page Street.

"Look, I'm with my fiancée now—when do you expect me to go back on the Eurostar?"

"We need you to get back tomorrow morning, with your fiancée. There is a small window of time before the charges against Miles Cooper are formalised. We want him to acknowledge the disappearance of Mr Bonham."

"I see your point inspector. I'll call you later this afternoon." The call ended, my instinctive reaction was to help out, albeit with serious risks. But I was used to taking those risks now…

Nancy emerged again, excited more than the previous time. "This one is amazing, but you are right, number two was also stunning, the embroidery was unique. But I can't rule out dress number one, what a creation! Which one do I choose?"

"I've got a good idea darling, but there is a request I need to make."

"Oh yes, what is it?" she asked, sitting next to me.

"Why don't I buy you all three dresses and the shoes we saw across the street?"

"What! You're amazing! But that's going to cost a lot, I mean a lot!" she said.

"It's no issue; it's my way of saying thank you. However, Scotland Yard needs us back in London tomorrow morning. It's to do with the ongoing investigation."

"Oh…I knew this trip was too good to be true! It's not every day the French police put you up in a luxury hotel!" She cried. "On the other hand, I think I've done all my shopping."

"Great!" I said. "Why don't you choose one more thing? I need to make an urgent call." A swift smile appeared on Nancy, and she began eyeing up what remained in the store. I called Inspector Hardcastle.

"Inspector, it's Josh. I'll do it. What are the instructions?"

"We don't want to endanger you any more than is necessary. This time we want you to go to Page Street and show them the passport obtained by Miles. We need a clue, anything, any lead we can get to identify its origin, the maker, where it has been?"

"So, let me get this straight. I'll show them the passport. They tell me some information, or not as the case might be. That's it?"

"Yes, it's that simple. The main thing is you don't want to arouse any suspicion. If that happens, then you are in severe danger," the inspector warned. "Also, we'll send you a credit card to use. Its purpose is twofold; it'll help us trace the monetary transactions from their dodgy card machine, and it also contains a microphone. It's best if I email you the instructions; you must go over them for your own safety. When you arrive at Kings Cross tomorrow, we will have an unmarked police taxi waiting for Nancy. You will use the tube system to make your way to Pimlico, and from there straight to Page Street. Do you understand? One other thing—as far as anyone is concerned, you are still Mr Bonham. Your Eurostar tickets will be booked under this identity and you are not to use your real passport. You should have no problems at passport control on your return."

"Yes inspector."

"I'll send the instructions in a short while. The police credit card and Miles' copy of Mr Bonham's passport will be given to you at the hotel reception."

"Okay thanks, goodbye," I said, looking up at Nancy, who was now wearing a turquoise jumpsuit.

"Perfect for summer isn't it?"

After the indulgent afternoon of designer shopping, we took a break at a corner café. Our pavement table gave a triple aspect view of all the roads meeting at this corner, and I detailed the conversation I had had with Inspector Hardcastle, minus the payment of ten thousand pounds for fake ID.

"I can see how it is a necessary evil that you need to get involved again. This poor man has probably been murdered. His family needs to know what happened to him," Nancy agreed.

"Yes, that was my reaction. Omega must get to the bottom of this mess—one of their employees has caused it all! I'm in a position to help, and I should." Glad that Nancy saw my perspective, we walked back to the hotel, both carrying bags in each hand. At the reception desk, there was an envelope waiting for me as the inspector had promised. The remainder of the day was spent at the hotel spa, after which we boarded a river cruise for dinner.

Chapter 18
Remember Me?

Nancy and I took the Eurostar back to London on Wednesday morning. On the train, I re-read the instructions that the inspector had given. There was a list of questions, organised in a flow diagram like structure. One question led to another and depending on what little information was possibly thrown my way. I then had to follow it up with a further probing question. However, all of it was entirely conjecture, as the guy on Page Street might refuse to open the door!

The announcement on the train stated we were ten minutes from our destination. Nancy knew the plan. She would look out for the taxi driver holding her name plaque, who would be an officer from Scotland Yard. She was to return home, but with an armed guard until the operation was over. The train pulled into the platform, and we got off.

"Mr Bonham, do look after yourself," she said.

"Yes darling. I pretty much know what I have to say. I should be back soon after you."

"What should I say to Chela? I mean she knows you weren't shot in Paris. I couldn't lie to her."

"That's fine. I know she won't say anything. Anyway, I'm looking forward to being back home…a cup of tea would be nice!"

"Sure. Once you're back in the apartment, I think I'm going to confiscate all your passports so there will be no crazy trips going forward!"

I smiled and gave her a hug. We then went on our separate journeys as planned. I took the short tube ride to Pimlico station, conscious that I hadn't stepped outside the train network to see what the weather was like. I was pleased to emerge from Pimlico station on a bright but blustery day. It felt good to walk the streets of my city, although I wasn't heading home for now. Inspector Hardcastle's words kept repeating in my head, 'You don't want to arouse any suspicion'. That was the key thing, to remain calm and keep to the script that I had been given.

I approached Page Street from the opposite direction this time around. I knew exactly where I was going, and without even thinking turned towards the refuse area. The grubby blue door was within sight, and I was relatively calm. I knocked on the door and unsurprisingly there was no reply the first time around. I knocked again, knowing I had been watched as I approached.

"It's Josh Rosenburg, I need to speak to you," I said.

"Josh who?" came a man's reply.

"Josh Rosenburg. I was here about a week ago, you gave me some ID, remember?"

"What do you want? We don't do refunds so get lost!" shouted the man.

"Look, I need some information. I'm willing to pay good money; I'm working undercover, as you know." There was a short delay, and then the door opened. The unforgettable stench from the flat wafted out as I entered inside. Staring at me was the short man I had spoken to last week; he was pointing a gun straight at me. My knee-jerk reaction was to put up my hands.

"I haven't got any weapons if that's what you're thinking," I said.

"We'll see about that," said the short man's accomplice. He moved towards me and started checking my outfit for any signs of a concealed weapon.

"Anything? Check for microphones and earpieces."

The accomplice carried out the orders, first demanding that I hand over my phone, but I replied I didn't have one. Then he made me take out all my possessions turning each pocket inside out and then asked me to remove my shoes to check them too. After a further minute of checks, he confirmed to the short man that I was clear and returned my belongings.

It seemed they were riled, an extra sense of paranoia filled the dark, foul-smelling interior of the room. "What do you want? People don't normally come back here. To be honest, the complete opposite—they go somewhere far away!"

"Well, as you know I have been posing as a Mr Bonham. But the real Mr Bonham is possibly dead. He is a client at my company, and the police suspect me. I need to find out what has happened to him."

"Why are you playing policeman?" he asked.

"I need to clear my name. If I don't find some kind of evidence to show them, I'll remain the prime suspect. I need to know what happened."

The short man sat down on a swivel chair and started typing on his laptop which was connected to two other computers in a tangle of cables. "So, are you saying you are still on the run?"

"Yes. I can't go around being myself at the moment. I've been discharged from work. If I use my phone, I could be traced. My passport is still blocked, I can't even travel. I'll get arrested at the first opportunity."

"Let me check if you are telling the truth." He typed into his laptop again. "So, I see your passport is still blocked by Interpol. But it looks like Mr Bonham has been to France. Nice trip?"

"Er, yes, great fine dining over there!" I replied. I'm sure he was looking at the passport record of me departing and returning to Kings Cross.

"So how can I help?"

"Well, on my investigations I came across a passport. It is also in the name of Mr Bonham. But it was made by the real mastermind of the fraud. The mastermind has possibly killed Mr Bonham."

"So, you want to catch a killer? And the killer has framed you?"

"In short, yes. In Paris, I tracked down this person, but he escaped and left behind some ID," I lied.

"And do you have this ID?"

"Yes, his passport. This is where I need your help. I need to know where it was made, possibly someone you may know of or have worked with. Also, I'm hoping you can tell me how long ago it was manufactured? I will pay for the information."

The short man didn't say anything. He was thinking it over and turned to his accomplice, who nodded.

"Okay. If I take a look at this passport and I don't know anything, I want £5,000 regardless. If I can tell you what you want, I will charge £10,000," he said.

I paused and thought about the instructions I had been given.

"Deal!" I exclaimed, pulling out the passport that Miles had left behind in the Pullman Hotel. Both men were instantly fixated on the cover as the short man opened the first page.

"Funny, I give people passports, not the other way around! It looks very good, very good indeed. But I'm the best at this!" he boasted. "Nobody is better than me!"

"I agree," I said.

"The cover page is excellent. The inside page with the photo is excellent. Now let me check the stamps." He was comparing Miles' passport to the one he had on his screen.

"Page three is good, page four is good, page five is good." He carried on slowly through each page, shining a special torch from underneath to view hidden watermarks. I was mildly impressed with his meticulous work ethic. I sat there, not saying a word as fifteen minutes passed. As I waited, the instructions from Inspector Hardcastle flowed through my mind. If you are sitting there, observe the surroundings, room measurements, sounds from adjacent rooms. Look for any vents or openings that could be a window or escape hatch. I discreetly took in the visual clues that were present.

My silent observations were interrupted by the short man. "Look at this…" he said very slowly, "page twenty-two." He held up the page to his accomplice with the torch firmly fixed to it. Then he laughed mockingly and his accomplice joined in, acting as if they had just heard the punch line from one of their favourite jokes. "What a useless idiot!"

The accomplice finally spoke. "I know that picture. I've seen that watermark before."

"Yes," agreed the short man. "It's Sergei, isn't it?"

"Yes," said the accomplice.

"Can you get one of Sergei's passports?" The accomplice went into another room and came back with a few samples, slapping them on the desk. "Yes, I thought as much. The same mistake on page twenty-two as the others. I know where it was made."

"You do?"

"Yes. But first the payment. Ten thousand please."

I took out the police credit card and passed it to him. Taking a brief squint at the card, he stuck it into the card machine. I entered the pin number and then we both waited.

"It's taking a bit longer than usual," he said, anxiously meeting my eyes.

"Oh, it's a new card, but the limit should be good." He looked at me suspiciously, but at that point, the transaction went through.

"So now I tell you. This rubbish passport was made by a guy called Sergei. He was based in South London until he was caught because of his mediocre workmanship," the short man gloated. Then turning to his accomplice. "Is Sergei still living at Her Majesty's pleasure?"

"Not sure," came the reply.

"Where was he exactly in South London?" I asked.

"Why is that so important?"

"Well, hopefully I can go there and ask some questions. I might be able to get hold of him."

"For your own sake, I wouldn't go unless you don't value your life. He is not as friendly as me! But since you ask, he ran his business on top of a fried chicken shop he owned on the Old Kent Road, opposite the Tesco's. I doubt anyone's there anymore."

"So when do you think this passport was made?"

"Good question. I like it—you take an interest in these things. The authorities change passports all the time; small changes that we don't notice, but they do. It helps them with their checks. I know this one is at least four years old."

"What can you tell from the watermarks?"

"No, that's when Sergei went to prison!" Both men sniggered loudly.

"Can you tell me Sergei's...."

"No! No more questions! You asked for information and I have given it."

"A surname, do you have his surname?"

"No, I don't. You have all the information I know." I thought for a second—had this man given enough clues, assuming they were accurate? Was he solely mocking me to earn a lucrative ten thousand for 30 minutes of work? I wasn't sure but my gut feeling told me he was genuine. Working in the field of client services I was attuned to when someone was being wary, false or frugal with the truth. This man had opened up to me, however minutely, and I could see he was a talkative individual. Unfortunately, his choice of profession didn't lend itself to utilising that particular skill. I guessed I could extract a bit more information from him. It was now or never.

"Thank you for the information. I believe you when you say you are the best."

"I am the best. That's why I charge a lot," he said.

"This Sergei guy—I know you can't tell me his surname, but do you have a photo of him? In case I go looking for help?"

"I told you, he's a vicious character. Don't blame me if you end up in the same graveyard as your client!" He hesitated, then did a quick internet search on his laptop. "If you look up 'Popular Food Centre' at the same location as the fried chicken shop I mentioned, there are some pictures of the owner. It is him;

he liquidated the food centre and then launched the chicken shop in its place. No more questions."

"Thank you," I said. "Can I have my passport back?"

"Yes, and remember my warning from last time," he said, not feeling the need to open the drawer with the gun.

"I understand. Thank you again." The accomplice opened the blue door, and I walked outside. The blustery weather had not died down, and I squinted to avoid dust entering my eyes, although the wind helped dispel the smell of the flat. *This is it,* I thought, *it's over*. I couldn't carry on doing this type of detective work. It had been a long week or so. I walked home, expecting a call or email from Scotland Yard when I arrived.

Chapter 19
Back at Chelsea Police Station

I entered my apartment block, grateful I had returned. The concierge smiled at me and I smiled back, but I continued walking, aiming not to answer any questions no matter how trivial. Opening the front door, I saw Nancy and the protection officer sitting in the lounge, discussing holiday destinations. I greeted them both and the officer stood up.

"Mr Rosenburg, I'm Officer Pelham. I'm sure it's been a bit stressful for you today, but Inspector Hardcastle says well done, you did a brilliant job. There's no need to talk to him today, but he wants you to report to the station tomorrow at 11:00 a.m. Is that ok?"

"Sure. It's not like I have a job to go to at the moment!" I replied.

"Oh, I was coming to that. He also said he has spoken to your company. They are aware that you no longer are a suspect and they'll email you about a return to work."

"Thank you. I was beginning to enjoy my break!"

The officer laughed. "One final thing before I go. Can you please hand over the police credit card?" I carried out her request, after which she left the apartment.

"Let me make you some tea," Nancy insisted. She disappeared into the kitchen, returning with a cup and saucer. "So, is it all over, Mr Bonham? Can I revert to calling you Josh?"

"I've done what I could; it's definitely over. Inspector Hardcastle wants to see me tomorrow, but I believe that's it." For the remainder of the day, Nancy and I stayed in watching TV and ordered a takeaway. The semblance of normality was much appreciated.

Conscious of the meeting at the police station at 11:00 a.m., I got ready early the next day. After breakfast, I began searching for news related to me and the fraud. There was only one update, which now suggested I was framed by someone who worked in finance and that the person shot in Sacre Coeur Montmartre was an accomplice of the real culprit, and not me. The details were vague; maybe Scotland Yard had censored the article. It mentioned I worked for Omega and that some kind of fraud had occurred, but there was no mention of Miles or the clients involved. I also searched for the food centre that the short man had mentioned. There wasn't much to see, apart from two guys standing outside the façade of a dreary looking shop with fruit and vegetables outside.

When it was time to go to the station, I ordered a cab and got there within five minutes. I was led straight into the interview room where Inspector Hardcastle was waiting.

"Morning Mr Rosenburg, nice to see you again."

"Morning, inspector."

"I'd like to start by saying you did an outstanding job yesterday. The microphone worked well, and we now have a major lead. Thanks for taking the time to read my instructions; we were aiming to get a photo or name, and you got both."

"So, was the passport guy telling the truth?"

"He was shockingly accurate. With his insight, we easily found who we were looking for. Sergei Chernenko is his full name, and he is still a tenant of HMS Belmarsh prison!"

"Sounds too good to be true!" I said.

"We are questioning him as we speak. He understandably doesn't remember making the passport for Miles as he's probably made quite a few in his time. But he does remember someone asking about a passport and a face mask. He has given us some dates, and we have narrowed the time frame to between four and a half years and five years ago. It fits in well with the disappearance of Mr Bonham. The good thing is that Sergei's premises above the chicken shop was on a main road, we should have a lot of video evidence we can follow up. I've got three detectives looking at tapes. I think we'll have a conviction on this very soon."

"That's brilliant. I mean it's sad to know Mr Bonham was probably murdered, but a conviction would be great. Omega needs to publish the bad news and move on. It has to overcome this as soon as possible."

"On that note, Scotland Yard will issue a statement to all the major media outlets in a private hearing this Sunday. This is a high-profile case, the French Embassy wants answers, the regulators are crawling all over Omega and Scotland Yard has a possible murder investigation on its hands. The police need to give a statement to the press, particularly in light of the misinformation we published about you."

"What implications will the press hearing have?"

"Well...we have to state that a fraudulent scheme was uncovered at Omega, and it is connected to an attempted murder of a client and the possible disappearance of another. We need to say that although you were the initial suspect, you went undercover to find the real criminal. It is important for us to mention you were on the run in Paris as that collaborates with the account from the French police. Hopefully, after the news is published, we may get further leads from the general public."

"Makes sense," I agreed.

The inspector continued. "To stop any further speculation by the media, we will also announce that Miles Cooper has been formally charged. So, unfortunately, the whole thing will be public by Sunday evening. Do you understand what I am saying?"

"Yes. I knew this was too big to keep quiet."

"The key thing is that this is an ongoing investigation, and nothing can be mentioned to the press or on social media. Any information about the case will be released by Scotland Yard and then at the trial, whenever that occurs."

"Understood," I said.

"Do you have any questions for me?"

"Yes. My main concern is the operation on Page Street. They know who I am and where I live. How can you guarantee there won't be any repercussions from them?"

"We are actively monitoring their operation 24 hours a day. They are inadvertently helping us solve a number of cases, as other criminals regularly use their services. So we are divided as to what to do with them. We could certainly use their know-how—they are one of the most skilled operators we've come across, particularly their ability in accessing secure databases."

"That's the impression I got inspector. If their skills were put to good use, they could be of great benefit. Plus, that cocky short chap was actually a likeable fellow."

"He's a clown!" said the inspector. "If you don't have any further questions, there are two more items I want to cover. Firstly, the French Embassy has reported that Mr Bertrand is improving, it'll be a while before he can talk to us, but we are hoping he can also give us information about Mr Bonham. The Embassy said you can't speak to him but feel free to call his wife if you want to pass on a message. By the way, Mrs Bertrand is privy to all of that which has been going on. Secondly, I've spoken to your CEO and mentioned we no longer need your assistance. He said you should return to work as normal on Monday morning. Any discussions about the fraud with unconnected members of staff at Omega are forbidden and there will be a separate investigation involving our financial crime unit. You'll hear more about that from the compliance officer at Omega."

"I see, acknowledged," I said.

"Any other questions please call me directly. I wish you a good day Mr Rosenburg and thank you again."

Hurriedly I left the police station, aiming to seize the opportunity to talk to Mrs Bertrand. I needed to speak to her given our last conversation, where she assumed I was to blame. On the way back to my apartment, I received an email from David Highfield. He congratulated me for helping with the investigation and confirmed my return to work. The email also mentioned that a separate workshop in conjunction with regulators and the police would be arranged. He reiterated the need for confidentiality and for business to resume as usual. I gathered that limiting reputational damage and fraud prevention were foremost on his mind. I wasn't sure how much he knew about my escapade in Paris, but then I don't think he would be interested either.

When I got home, I thought about what I should say to Mrs Bertrand. It was best for me to keep it brief, the poor woman must have gone through her fair share of anguish. I dialled Mr Bertrand's mobile number and Mrs Bertrand answered the call.

"Hello Mrs Bertrand, it's Josh Rosenburg."

"Afternoon Mr Rosenburg, I appreciate you calling, I hope you are well?" she asked.

"How is Alain?"

"I've been at the hospital every day. Alain has improved a lot, especially since he came out of the coma. He's still on a drip but alert and awake. He is not saying much but understands what I am telling him. The French police have spoken to him, but obviously, it is too early for an interview."

"That's good to hear," I said.

"The doctors say he should be back to normal in a fortnight or so."

"Oh, good. First of all, I want to apologise for the suffering that you and your family have been through. I wish things could have been different. Also, I can only apologise on behalf of my company."

"The Embassy told me, it's so scandalous. I would too like to say sorry, for assuming it could have been you given your name was in the papers. Had my husband been able to speak, he would have instantly defended your integrity. My family is extremely grateful to you for all your detective work and for taking it upon yourself to put things right."

"It's nothing, madam," I said. "The main driving force for me was to find out what happened and for justice to be done."

"It is too hard to believe. Hopefully, everything will get back to normal soon," she said.

"I'd like to pass on a message to Alain if I may. I wish him a speedy recovery and also tell him I owe him a lunch!"

"Sure, I will tell him. Mr Rosenburg, thank you."

"Thank you. Goodbye now," I said. The call was brief but immensely satisfying. I wasn't sure when I'd see Mr Bertrand again. I imagined he'd want to get back to France as soon as he was able to do so. Fortunately, he had survived the poisoning and was conscious again, but what about Mr Bonham? There was still more pain for someone to endure. All I could do was hope.

Epilogue

A relatively unexciting weekend was exactly what I needed. I spent Saturday making wedding arrangements with my local church and watching sports in the afternoon. Sunday was occupied with Nancy and me doing routine tasks around the apartment and cooking a roast dinner.

As I awoke on Monday morning, the first thought that dawned on me was my return to work. At breakfast, I checked my emails, there was one from the French police department. They had emailed to say I was eligible for a reward, stating a five-figure sum! I immediately told Nancy the good news.

"Wow, now I know why you were so generous in that clothing store in Paris!" she said.

I smiled. "I had no idea it was going to be so much!"

Having got dressed, Nancy and I were almost ready to leave the apartment when the sound of a crowd jeering and joking outside could be heard.

"Who is it this time?" Nancy asked.

"I think they're waiting for us," I replied. Nancy looked through the window to see a stream of reporters shoving each other in a time-honoured ritual, some with outstretched necks peering at our window.

"What shall we do, Josh? You're going to be on the front page!"

"Let's go to work!"

Entering the foyer, all appeared quiet, but journalists and photographers were loitering outside the main entrance. I nodded at the porter who opened the main door. The flash of bulbs and noise was incredible.

"Mr Rosenburg, how does it feel not being on the run?"

"Did you ever think that you were going to jail?"

"Is it easy to commit a crime like this?"

I stood at the entrance and thought I'd say a few words.

"I can't say too much as the investigation is still ongoing, but I'd like to say I'm glad to be back and returning to my employment at Omega Centurion. The

French and British police did a fantastic job and I'm indebted to them. It was scary being undercover and on the run in Paris, but the best bit was unmistakably the French cuisine! Have a good day!" We left the crowd behind us and commenced our walk towards Strutton Ground.

"I know you've been doing a lot of wedding shopping recently, darling, but I thought I'd just let you know to prepare for somewhere very hot."

"Oh, I see," Nancy said, trying not to seem too excited.

"Yes, and don't forget comfortable clothes for the flight, we may be in the air for a long time."

Then she came out with it. "Are we going to the Caribbean?"

"That's a very good guess," I said. She jumped up and down and gave me a huge hug. Some of the reporters who had been following us at an indiscreet distance took a few snaps. We continued our journey and kissed each other goodbye at our usual spot. Heading for St James's Park, I looked at my diary to double-check my schedule and began the preparation for my next client meeting.

It was another day.